INGE SCHILPEROORD

TENCH

Translated by David Colmer

PUSHKIN PRESS

LONDON

Pushkin Press
71–75 Shelton Street
London, WC2H 9JQ

Original text © Inge Schilperoord 2015
English translation © David Colmer, 2017

Published by special arrangement with Uitgeverij Podium in conjunction
with their duly appointed agent 2 Seas Literary Agency.

Tench was first published as *Muidhond* in Amsterdam, 2015

First published by Pushkin Press in 2017

1 3 5 7 9 8 6 4 2

ISBN 978 1 78227 234 2

N ederlands
letterenfonds
dutch foundation
for literature

This publication has been made possible with financial
support from the Dutch Foundation for Literature

Designed and typeset by Tetragon, London
Printed in Great Britain by the CPI Group, UK

www.pushkinpress.com

*...this confrontation between the human need
and the unreasonable silence of the world.*

ALBERT CAMUS, *THE MYTH OF SISYPHUS*
(translation by Justin O'Brien)

NOW I HAVE TO PAY attention, thought Jonathan. Now. It's starting now. He laid his trembling hands on his lap and rubbed the middle of his left thumb with his right in the hope that it would calm him down. It was his last morning in jail. Like always, he was alone in his cell. The cell the others, the guards, called his room. He was sitting on the bed waiting, staring at the wall. He didn't know what time it was. It was early, he knew that much. The first strip of sunlight had just forced its way through the split in the too-thin curtains. Half-five, maybe six o'clock. It didn't make any difference to him today. I've got time, he thought. From now on I've got plenty of time. They'll come when they come. When they think it's the right time, they'll come. I can't do anything about that. No earlier, no later. I'll see.

Until they came he would watch the morning light push further into his cell and slowly, imperturbably, move across the walls in its own orbit, ignoring everybody. It had been ages since he'd known exactly what time it was. The first night here he'd immediately fiddled the batteries out of the wall clock. He couldn't stand the ticking. Plus the clock didn't tell him anything that was any use to him. Day activities weren't compulsory and he didn't sign up for any of them. Walking in circles, education, sport. Work. If you didn't smoke, eat sweets or buy expensive clothes, you didn't need any money here.

He preferred to watch the position of the sun, the fullness of the light, the way it caught the clouds drifting over the watchtowers. That told him how much longer it was going to last, how long till dark. How much longer he'd have to put up with the racket: men's voices creeping up from the exercise yard, music through the walls. Shadows across the floor of his cell, across the bed and the small table. But now it was going to be different. "Everything will be different," he whispered.

He waited. It was still quiet outside. After a while he stood up, walked from the bed to his table, from the table to the window, stood there for a moment and went back to his bed. He sat down again, knees creaking quietly, then stood up once more. He paused in the middle of his cell, then went back to the table and looked down at it. On it were his therapy workbook, his exercise book, pencils and pens. The bookmark his mother had sent him. He sat down at the table again, his back straight, and opened the exercise book. A beautiful, blank page. He used both hands to smooth it out, arranged it in the exact middle of the table, unscrewed the lid of his pen and thought for a moment. After what seemed like ages it turned out he couldn't think of anything sensible to write. He nibbled at the inside of his cheek. Why not? Why should he run dry today?

He stood up again and clenched his fists. Walked from his table to the window, from the window to the table and back again. He sat down on the chair. "Nothing," he wrote. And then, "Never." Followed by, "No!" He banged the exercise book shut. The rest would come tonight when he was back home. He'd do the next therapy assignment then. A little later he opened the exercise book again, stared at what he'd written and crossed it out. "Different," he wrote beneath it, then drew a line through that too. "Better."

He rolled up the exercise book, picked up his pens and pencils one at a time and put them in his pencil case, and slipped the workbook into his bag with the rest. Then he sat down on the bed, hands trembling on his lap, and waited for the moment when the guard would unlock the door.

Now I have to pay attention, thought Jonathan. Now. It's starting now. He was sitting next to the last window, at the back of the bus to the village. There weren't any other passengers, but he'd still walked past the empty seats. There was quite a bit of morning left to go: the sun was still rising, but it was already terribly hot. A drop slid out from his hair, slowly, down his neck. All the way to the small of his back. He shifted on the seat. He had his bag on his lap, holding it close. He was sweating under his arms too. The bag was heavy on his knees. He would have preferred to put it down on the floor, but somehow it seemed safer like this, his fingers tightly intertwined. He sighed.

Between him and the world was the glass and behind the glass the coastal landscape. The most beautiful country he knew. The place where he had crawled out of his mother's womb on a nondescript Sunday morning some thirty years ago. A place he would never leave. He looked at the landscape with brand-new eyes. Not a single detail escaped him. He saw the tops of the pine trees and the way the sun was very precisely spotlighting the last row of sandhills, the grass on the side of the road and the water of the small pools in the distance. The light slid along the road with the bus, heating the asphalt. It was so hot it wouldn't have surprised him to see the tar bursting open in front of him, starting to crack and melting from the inside out. Soft, sticky lumps like mud on the soles of his shoes.

He closed his eyes for a moment, reopened them and looked at the sky again. The light was almost painful, such a glaring white.

Past the water tower, the bus curved off and down to the right before slowly climbing again after the next bend. He knew it all by heart, able to predict every twist and bump in the road. Just a couple of minutes to the harbour, he thought, and then the village. He could smell the slight stink of the sea air through the open roof hatch. Fish, oil, decay, seaweed. Rope.

This afternoon he would be out walking in these dunes, maybe within an hour. At last. People didn't like him; they never had. But nature accepted him as he was. He squeezed one hand with the other, held it like that, then stretched the fingers one at a time until he heard the knuckles crack. His mother would be home waiting for him. Sitting on the sofa, where else, watching morning TV. He could almost hear the sound of the set that had been about to give up the ghost for years now. All those nights sitting next to her on his regular chair, the smell of the dog in the room. Her hands clasped together and resting just under her bosom. Often he'd be reading *Nature* magazine but unable to keep his mind on the words, the TV voices stabbing into his thoughts. Then he'd let the magazine slip down to his lap and watch her watch TV.

He thought about the little things, the things he knew so well. The way the fingers of her right hand curled together and slowly, absently reached for the thin chain of her necklace, the way she took the silver cross between thumb and index finger and began to rub it. That meant that something on TV had aroused her interest and she was about to draw his attention to it. The way she let the rosary beads glide through her fingers when she was praying at night.

His hands were clammy. He felt the warmth of the engine rumbling away inside the bus. Now and then he looked at his nails, tugging at little bits of skin. Sometimes he raised himself up slightly to get a better look into the distance, squinting against the glare, then sitting down again.

He watched the seagulls gliding through the sky with their beaks open. Sometimes they hung motionless for a moment as if frozen in place. He thought of the birds whose flight he had watched through his cell window. As long as he could. The powerful beating of their wings. When they sailed past close to his window, he imagined he could hear the wind whooshing across their quills. In the back of his exercise book he kept a list of unusual birds. Kittiwake gulls, lesser black-backed gulls, fulmars, a guillemot. Tallying them gave him some peace of mind amid the racket, the endless suffocation. It was unbearable. Especially the proximity of all those men. The nauseating smell of food.

But it was over now, as suddenly as it had begun. Despite everything it had felt sudden. Last week was the umpteenth hearing: the whole day in the docks, his lawyer's words going straight over his head like always.

And yesterday afternoon the official letter from the court arrived. He had been acquitted on appeal. After all. Despite his worst fears. That cancelled out everything: the prison sentence, the therapy, the psychiatric hospital. There wasn't enough evidence. They hadn't been able to find the T-shirt on which, in the words of the prosecutor, incriminating traces could be found according to the victim's statements. "The prosecution can still appeal," his lawyer explained, "but I don't expect them to." The case would only be reopened if they could dig up some more evidence. But that was anyone's guess. For the time being he was free.

He swallowed painfully. As if there was something hard and sharp, a fish bone, caught in his throat. He coughed, sighed, closed his eyes and flared his nostrils. He concentrated on his breathing to try to stop his shoulders tensing up. That was what he'd learnt in pre-therapy, as they called it. Or "individual offender therapy", therapy that started in prison and was meant to prepare him for treatment in the hospital. It had begun a few weeks ago with the prison psychologist. Phase one.

"Take a calm breath," he whispered to himself, looking at the vague silhouette of his face in the window, the sharp chin and high cheekbones, his forehead. "In through the nose." He closed his eyes for a moment and opened them again. "Hold it, and then slowly, slowly, out through the mouth." He repeated this ten times, always ten times. "In this way we relax the diaphragm and let all stress fall away. Feet on the ground." He kept whispering, even though he was still the only passenger on the bus. He felt his diaphragm relaxing, his breath growing calm, and meanwhile he massaged his tense and painful neck muscles with his knuckles.

The bus rounded the last bend before the village. Clustered around the long main street was the new estate he'd heard so much about, the houses silent in the morning light, their windows reflecting the sunbeams straight back at him, dazzling him, as if deliberately. He averted his eyes: looking down at his feet, at his bag and off to the side instead. The estate had been tacked onto the old village in the past few months and, in a few weeks, he and his mother would come to live here too. She'd written about it all the time in her letters. New neighbours, a new house: she was so happy ("new faces for a change, a bit of life on the streets, people to talk to"). Not him. He didn't like change.

What he saw was worse than he had imagined. Rows and rows of narrow, identical houses. Short shadows between the roofs. They would be living in each other's pockets, here even more than in the old streets he was used to. Their own neighbourhood, the oldest part of the village, was earmarked for clearance months before Jonathan left. But the council was so slow nobody believed it was really going to happen. Then, while he was in jail, things had picked up speed after all. The first residents left during his second month and the rest followed in dribs and drabs. His mother was now the only one left and the other houses had all been knocked down. In her letters she had written that her asthma had grown worse over the last few months and she was too weak to organize the move by herself.

He pressed the button and a little later the bus stopped and the doors sighed open. He focused on his breathing again and then on the road, stretching slowly ahead. This was what he had looked forward to all these months. The enormousness of the sky, empty except for a few wisps of cloud. He looked straight up and let his eyes wander without any bars, bricks or towers to stop them. Long beams of sunlight on the road. He looked at the fishermen's cottages that had been spared as yet, their roofs and gardens, the top of the church tower. Here and there he could see fishing rods and baskets, small upturned boats against the front walls. Behind them, trees.

It was a clear day and oppressively humid. Much too hot for the time of year. He thought about the *Nature* magazines his mother had sent him faithfully every month with one of her letters. Always with the same sentence written on the label in her angled cursive: "For my boy, and may he come home soon." A few weeks ago he had read that the persistent heat had led to the first nests of brown-tail moth caterpillars being spotted in the sea buckthorn, much too early. Maybe the wood small-reed had already started flowering as well. "See," he'd mumbled to himself in his cell while sliding the magazine into the therapy folder he kept under his mattress. "See, it's not right. You can't even count on nature any more. Everything's out of kilter."

*

Their house was small, even smaller than he remembered it. It now stood with just one other house on the edge of a bare expanse. Apart from a few withered shrubs, some bricks and the odd bit of building debris, there was nothing here at all. The entire block of fishermen's cottages next to theirs had simply disappeared. The high-rises were gone too. The two blocks of flats had disappeared into thin air as if they'd never even existed. As if his memory of them wasn't real. But he could still picture it all, every last detail. Elizabeth lived on the third floor of the second block. The whole neighbourhood called her Betsy. Him too. But never out loud.

He could still see her hanging over the railing of her balcony to wave at people passing by. He heard her thin, high voice. "Hello, Frank—Hello, Mum—Hello, Jon." He stared at a spot in the silent, shimmering air and for a second it was like she was walking there. With her big awkward head bobbing gently, as always. Her round face and sweet smile. Her mouth always slightly open.

He looked around, as if she might still be wandering some-where among those dry stubby shrubs. She was long gone, of course. After what happened, she and her parents had moved to the city. He stayed standing there awhile, squinting in the blazing sun. There was a glitter to the light and, for a moment, the emptiness around him seemed to give off a strange murmur. He felt a chill of fear at the sight of their house surrounded by a wasteland of demolition. As if it was all wrong. As if he didn't belong here. As if he belonged somewhere completely different. But he didn't have a clue where that might be or how to find out.

Between the brick walls of their squat house it was, if possible, even hotter than outside. His mother was waiting for him in the steaming-hot kitchen, wearing the summer blouse she had owned as long as he could remember. It was small and stretched tight around her bosom.

"There's my boy."

"Mum."

He smiled a bit; she smiled, but he didn't greet her the way he had hoped, the way he'd intended. Not even the way he'd nervously, expectantly imagined these last few days by the window of his cell. He was too cautious, too hesitant.

"You're back." Her eyes gleamed. He smiled again, a little shy, uncomfortable in this situation. Her boy. He sniffed, as if he was still ten and not thirty. He needed to give her a big grin; that was what he'd decided beforehand. But his face muscles felt stiff and weren't cooperating. He tried again. She had been alone all this time, he thought, and he was to blame. Now he needed to make it up to her. The least he could do was be a little bit friendly.

They stood there silently facing each other in the small room under the gaze of the earthenware statue of Mary that had been standing there on a shelf since his childhood. Quietly, with her hands folded and her eyes half closed, she looked down at the ground. As if searching for something she'd lost. Like always her glance passed them by. No matter how much his mother prayed to her and lovingly dusted her feet, she had never turned her eyes upon them.

They stood there like that for a while, the sweat running down his back. The air in the room was almost unbreathable. The house seemed to have got damper. He'd noticed the wallpaper in the hall peeling and blistering and the lino was starting to curl up along the joins.

"Jonny, at last. Thank God. I thought you'd never..." She didn't finish her sentence. He could hear a rustling in her voice.

"I'm here now."

She hadn't visited him once in all those months. He hadn't wanted her to: it would have been too much. He couldn't have borne seeing her there in that echoing visiting hall with all those other people. For a while she'd tried to insist, but in the end she gave up.

He wiped the sweat from his neck and out of his eyes with his sleeve and turned more towards her to see her better. For a moment he thought something was changing in her face. The muscles around her mouth tightened; he was scared she was going to cry. But nothing happened. She just raised her necklace between her thumb and index finger, then gently released it so it fell back against her throat.

He could tell that her asthma had taken a toll. Her skin had lost some of its elasticity and was covered with fine, almost invisible crazing, shallow lines over her face that came together in a slight frown above her nose. She hoped, as he knew from her letters, that it would get better again in the new house, which she was expecting to be less damp. But now he'd seen how hurriedly and cheaply the new homes had been thrown together, he knew it would be just as bad there as it was here.

Silence filled the room, with just the quiet hum of TV reaching him from the living room. He cleared his throat and wondered if he should hug her after all. His arms around her shoulders, her familiar smell. But he didn't; his muscles froze at the thought of it. He just reached out to her, with one hand moving towards her arm—hesitant, unsure—then he pulled it back again.

"Did you have a good trip?" she asked. "How did the trip go? Did you have enough money on you?"

"You already know that." He twisted the corner of the hankie he'd pulled out of his pocket, used it to wipe his throat and, without looking at her, repeated himself. "You already know that. They gave me a ticket. I already told you."

"Shall I make you a cuppa?"

She took a step towards him and spread her hands, presenting her empty palms like a sign of appeasement, a promise that she wouldn't ask him any difficult questions. Ever. Or at least, not yet. Before he could say anything, she continued, "Was the bus on time? Did you have something to eat with you?"

"It's not far, Mum. Half an hour at most. You know that."

She was just asking to have something to ask. Like in her letters. She never asked him about the case. And he never said anything about it either. She couldn't *not* know what he'd been convicted of, and acquitted. But her letters were about moving, the weather, Bible quotes. And he wrote to her about things he'd read in *Nature*, about the birds he'd seen.

"Would you like some squash instead? A nice glass of squash?" She bent down towards the low fridge, drawing his gaze to the worktop. Although it was already quite late in the morning, it was still cluttered with the mess from breakfast. By the looks of it the cutlery and dishes from the previous evening hadn't been washed up yet either.

"I'm going to the dunes."

"Already?"

"I have to get out for a bit."

"Have a drink first."

He felt the tendons in his neck tighten as the tension returned to his muscles. He stretched his head back and heard a dry click when his neck cracked. He combed the sweaty hair away from his forehead with the fingers of both hands. He was suddenly desperate to be alone.

"Has Milk been out yet? Otherwise I'll take him with me." There was a moist layer on his throat and back. "There's no air in here." He moved his hands as if defining the area the air was being sucked out of. At the same time he heard his own words and realized that his voice didn't sound friendly. Picking at the collar of his shirt, he tried again. "I'm going out for a little walk—you can understand that, can't you?"

"Yes, of course, just go ahead, son. He hasn't been out yet, just in the yard."

He found the leash hung over the door handle like always and saw through the open door how messy the living room was. There were playing cards in crooked piles in the most unlikely places, scraps of paper, brochures, a rosary, her Bible.

He sighed and his stomach shrank. Something for later, he thought. One step at a time. I'll tidy up soon. I'll make it all spic and span. I'm a champ at that. But first, outdoors.

Restlessly he ran the leash through his fingers and called the dog with a short, sharp whistle. "Milk!"

"You won't be late back, will you?"

He said he'd keep his eye on the time. It flashed through his mind that she talked too much. He'd never been able to stand it, but now he wasn't used to it at all. He liked to keep words to a minimum. All too often they only caused trouble.

Again she told him to drink enough. Again he said yes. She turned, took a plastic bottle out of the kitchen cupboard and filled it with water. "You can top it up at the pump in the dunes."

He could almost feel her squeaking, laboured breathing in his own lungs. Although he didn't want to, he thought about prison. The looks the other men gave him whenever he left his cell to get something to eat. The constant fear that the guards would be distracted for a moment. Waiting for the inevitable. Never before had he been so scared. Terrified every single day. The unrelenting fear that he wouldn't be able to stand it any longer. But still the time kept slipping past.

Through the television voices he heard the soft click of nails approaching from behind the half-open door to the living room. The old dog strolled up to him on his crooked legs, tongue lolling out.

"Milk," he said softly. Unexpected tears leapt to his eyes like tiny needles. To keep them back he cleared his throat, and again, and squatted down. The dog stopped for a moment and held his head at an angle, as if to see him better, then walked up to him, stretched out his neck and began licking him on the face with big long slurps, tail wagging.

"Oh, boy. Down, boy," he laughed. He gave the dog a good scratch all over and heard a deep growl of satisfaction. Then pressed his cheek against the dog's warm, glowing flank, while moving his hands quickly over his short, wiry hair. He grabbed both his ears. "You coming out with me, buddy? You coming?" Milk gave a short, high bark and sauntered along behind him.

He quickly took his bag upstairs first, standing motionless in the middle of the small room of hardly ten square metres where he had lived his entire life. It looked gloomier than he remembered. The angled rafters, the low light. The empty aquarium below the window in the corner. He had to fill it as soon as possible; it made him nervous straight away. He knew he wouldn't really feel at home until there were fish in the tank.

He'd always had fish. His mother was completely indifferent to them, but they calmed him down. Their slow, placid circling, the way their fins glided through the water. It was like they were gulping away chunks of time for him, reducing something he'd never known what to do with. As far back as he could remember he'd had that vague anxiousness about how to get through the day, how to fill the hours. From the moment he got home from work, the period until it was time to go to bed seemed like an unbridgeable void.

"Don't dawdle," he told himself. "Come on, get outside now you finally can." He put his bag on the bed, but a moment later he'd knelt down in front of the aquarium. It was filthy. He couldn't leave it like that.

He fetched a bucket and washing-up liquid from the tiny bathroom next to his bedroom and scrubbed the greasy spots off the glass as best he could while the dog circled restlessly on the carpet, whining under his breath.

"Lie down, boy," he said. And when there was no reaction: "Down!" But the dog refused. Jonathan looked at him, at his funny drooping ears, his quivering nose. All at once it was like his limp had got worse. With one hand on the dog's back, he gently pushed him down onto the floor. He stayed there but kept up his quiet whimpering.

Jonathan used his scraper to quickly scratch the algae away from the edges, washed out the bottom of the tank and checked his old pump to see if it still worked. He connected it and used his pocketknife to scrape off some rust spots while he was waiting. Eventually the pump coughed and spluttered and began blowing a feeble but steady stream of bubbles through the dirty water.

He put the dog on the leash and left through the back door, walking quickly with his shoulders hunched and his head down. Although he couldn't see anyone out on the street, he felt like he was being watched. He hurried past the back gardens of the houses on the edge of the village in the direction of the sea. The sun was still beaming down in an otherwise empty sky, weighing down on the earth. Soon he was wandering through the sandhills he'd been visiting his whole life and the dog was trotting along obediently behind him, though panting heavily.

It had been so long since he'd been here and he could feel how much he would have been enjoying it if not for his thoughts about jail. He tried to shake them off, moving his head gently. Every now and then he stopped for a moment on the path through the dunes, under the empty dome of the sky, to breathe in the smells of the earth, and cautiously, gradually, he managed to stop brooding.

In the corner of his eye he saw the dog looking up at him expectantly, hoping that he'd throw a stick or take him swimming in a pond or just lie down for a nap somewhere, like so often before. "Soon, boy," he said, "soon."

He kept looking up, tilting his head, peering into the endless sky. "Look, Milk," he whispered, "look." The sun was fierce, aiming its merciless heat at the earth with an intensity he was no longer used to. The perspiration dripped from his cheeks. He pushed further and further into the dunes, relishing everything, every smell, every little rustling sound, as if he was brushing against it all, reminding the things around him who he was, that he was back. The jagged hawthorn branches silhouetted against the sky, the special smell of the pines, the sand, the water of the small ponds.

He lay down in a hollow next to a small pool, closed his eyes and almost immediately opened them again because he thought he'd heard something. There was nobody there. He felt a slight breeze on his skin, heard the reeds rustling behind his back. This was the dry quiet. What he'd been waiting for through every filthy second of those endless days and nights. To be back here in familiar territory, alone with the dog. He took his water bottle, raised it to his lips, then poured some into a cupped hand for the dog, feeling the rough tongue on his skin. After drinking, Milk lay down next to him. He reached out and scratched him on the head, then stayed like that for a long time, enjoying every moment in that dome of warmth.

He felt a ridiculous urge to pray, to do something to show his gratitude, but he couldn't believe in any of that, despite his mother's best efforts. He thought of the sign of the cross she'd made just before he left. She'd traced an imaginary cross on his forehead. He sniffed. Even before they'd locked him up, he'd lost his faith. Nobody could prove that any of it was true. It wasn't scientific like the programme of treatment he was participating in. That was based on data, statistics.

Since the pre-therapy started more than a month ago, he'd had a weekly session with the prison psychologist. And every day he did an assignment from his workbook. Even if he didn't understand all of the psychologist's explanations, the terms he used were promising: relapse-prevention plan, early-warning system. The programme they'd given him was full of boxes with short explanations of how he had to behave. What was good and what wasn't; where the risks lay. Thanks to this programme he was in the middle of a process of fundamental change.

"You really are doing your best, Jonathan. You are so motivated," the psychologist said. "I don't get many like you." And he'd looked straight at him with his pale eyes.

At first Jonathan had been uncomfortable in his presence. It had been a long time since someone had called him by his first name and been so friendly to him.

Fortunately, he'd been allowed to take his therapy book home with him to carry on by himself. He thought about the telephone call from his lawyer, just over a week ago. There wasn't enough forensic evidence, he said. Inconsistencies in the story. The victim hadn't been able to tell them very much. "Victim"—that word stung every time he heard it. He didn't want to think about it.

"You'll be on provisional release," his lawyer said, and before he knew it he was out on the street. After getting up this morning, he had stood for a while in front of the black-speckled mirror over the sink in his cell, staring at himself in disbelief, his head spinning from all the things he was thinking. All the things he was feeling but couldn't name.

When Jonathan began walking again he concentrated on the strength he felt in his body. In his fibres, his muscles, thighs and back. Like a child he ran part of the way up a sandhill. He wanted to feel elated, but it kept getting hotter and his limbs grew heavier. He kept wiping new beads of sweat from his forehead with the back of his hand.

He walked on for a long time, until the sun started to exhaust him, then napped for a while in a dip in the dunes with the dog before deciding to go past the old sandpit on the way back. He'd been going there his whole life to fish. It was the only pond in the dunes with brackish, almost fresh water. Home to perch, rudd and eels. If you were lucky, even a carp or a pike.

A few low, raggedy clouds had appeared in the sky. They were reflected in the water as they floated over. For a moment he thought he heard something and pricked up his ears. Was something rustling in the marram grass? He kept quiet and looked around but there was nothing. In the sky only seagulls slowly gliding past. Their shadows sweeping over the water.

He walked over to the bank, pushing aside reeds that pricked his arms and scraped over his shirt. With the dog behind him he cleared a path to the water's edge, where he leant forwards to get the sun behind him so he could see through the water. After peering at the bottom for a while, he moved even closer and saw some movement. Dark spots drifting slowly over the bottom of the pond, bigger than anything he'd ever seen here before. They had to be fish, but what kind? While he stared at them intently, he felt his heart trembling with excitement. The large shadows slid slowly back and forth, left and right over the bottom. From the corner of his eye he saw that the dog had walked a few metres away and was snuffling around a clump of grass close to the water's edge before disappearing back into the reeds. The splash told him that he had jumped into the water and was now in the pond.

Jonathan turned his attention back to the dark shapes. "Hey," he said, hearing his own voice again after what felt like ages. "Hey, who are you?" Pushing the reeds further apart with his elbows, he bent even lower. A line of tiny bubbles was winding up out of the depths. "Hey, where have you come from?"

They were big fish, that was clear, but he couldn't identify them. Maybe carp stirring up the silt in search of food, but he was too far away to be sure. He'd always wanted carp in his aquarium. Just the idea of it made him want to go straight home to get his rod, but from the position of the sun he guessed it had already gone half-three and he'd promised his mother he'd do the shopping: meat, potatoes, bread, wine. She'd given him some money. Could he run home, fetch his rod, catch a fish and set up his aquarium this evening? He quickly did the calculations: home at four, half-four back here, wait, catch, walk back, five o'clock, no, half-five—that'd be too late. He clenched his fists and heard the words of his psychologist: "You're someone who acts first and thinks later. We're going to reverse that."

He straightened up and stood there for a moment. Now I have to pay attention, he thought. Now. It's starting now. He breathed out with little puffs. Tomorrow morning. I have to do it tomorrow morning. It's Sunday, I don't have to work until Monday. If he used his biggest rod he should be able to manage it.

*

With long strides he hurried back to the village by way of the highest sandhill, stopping for a moment on the top. In the distance was the sea, a motionless expanse, with a few lonely container ships here and there on the horizon. In front of him he could already see the rooftops looming up. Houses, people, all the streets identical, every face the same. He lowered his head down between his shoulders and concentrated on the sound of his own breath. He counted his steps. One, two, three, four, five, six, seven, eight, one, two, three, four. Now and then he glanced up for a second, before returning his gaze to the paving stones.

He couldn't bear people. They didn't talk to him. They didn't know him. They went by the whispers in the alleys. Even the roofs of the houses seemed to be leaning towards each other like conspirators, as if they too were enjoying the gossip. The streets were entangled, with the biggest all ending at the square with the church, whose meddlesome tower and spire looked out over everything. Fortunately, nobody was out on the streets right now.

Just outside the village, at the supermarket in the harbour, where it was always busy and he could avoid the villagers, he bought some bacon and the rest of the shopping. Then he sat down on a bench for a moment. He thought about the therapy that was going to turn him into a different person. Module 1 was finished; four more to go. A different person. A new person. He pondered it. Could he become new? He had never felt new. His shoulders were aching as if he'd been lugging heavy baskets of fish offal around the factory. He looked at his hands, lying on his knees. The fingers, short and bent, were tense, the skin tight, small wounds here and there. Now there was the scar above his lip as well. He'd have to make do with this body for years to come, trying to keep out of trouble.

Soon he'd stick his key in the lock and hear the murmur of the television. Sitting across from his mother at the table, too close. A game of cards, listening to her mumbling the scores to herself, the words of the verses she reads in her old Bible. Watching TV, making some coffee. He stayed sitting there a little longer, picking at the quick of his nails.

He was in the kitchen standing at the worktop. His mother was sitting on a chair by the window and playing cards against herself. Patience. It was almost half-four and as hot as when the sun had been at its highest. The window was open. Not a breath of wind. The back of his shirt was stuck to his skin.

The worktop was still a mess. Cutlery everywhere, glasses with greasy stains and the dregs of wine. He filled the sink with suds, gave everything a good scrub and put the shopping on the freshly scoured worktop. The bread, the bag of potatoes, the meat. He laid the sharpest knife and spatula out ready, then cleared out the kitchen cupboards, washed and dried them, refilled them and started to peel the potatoes.

Now he was back home, he would cook every day again. He liked that: fixed activities, fixed times. And he was good at looking after other people. When he'd had to write down his strengths in the workbook, he'd considered this one of his best qualities. Caring for others.

He thought back on the IQ test he'd done for the psychologist. They'd explained that in some areas he was a bit weaker than average. But in others his mind was actually very well developed. His eye for detail, for instance. That was useful now. Sunk in thought like this he'd almost forgotten his mother; now he felt her presence again. Occasionally she would mumble something or hum a quiet, almost monotone tune. Putting cups or plates away in the cupboard, he saw her wipe the sweat from her face with a hankie in her left hand while keeping score with her right. He tried not to let her presence disturb him too much. After a while she took the dog into the living room with her, stretched out on the sofa and called out, "Jon, why don't you come in here?"

Taking the pan with him, he sat down on a stool across from her. The TV was on, like always. With short, quick movements back towards his body, he peeled the potatoes with the knife. With a splash the smooth, naked spuds landed in the pan one after the other. His mother was so close he had to sit at an angle to avoid bumping knees. He slid back a little.

She was watching a quiz show that only bored him and had already poured herself some wine. Every now and then she'd reach over to the side table. A couple of rectangular ice cubes were floating just below the rim of the glass.

By five he had everything prepared and a half-hour left to do an assignment. That was enough. In prison he'd done one a day, now he wanted to do two. He felt himself glowing from within at that resolution. "You're a hard worker," the psychologist had said, and hard work was extra important now.

He went upstairs. The old steps creaked under his feet. He could feel the splintering wood through his socks. He sat on the bed with his back to the wall and his arms wrapped around his legs, took a deep breath and stared ahead for a moment, before taking his workbook out from under his pillow and clamping it between his legs. He looked around the room: his bed, the chair, the small table, the aquarium. On the bedside cabinet there was a pen tray with two pens, a pencil and a rubber, a lamp, a box of tissues and a travelling alarm clock with a luminescent face. Nothing on the walls. In prison other men had pinned up posters and photos from magazines on the walls of their cells.

Not him. Even as a child he'd loved emptiness and hated clutter. He'd always put all his money into fishing gear. He listened to the silence for a moment, then opened the workbook and began.

The first assignment was called "First-line help with anger and tension" and featured a chart with solutions to help "escape stressful situations". "Leaving and doing a relaxation exercise," he read, "asking for help, going for a walk." He had to add a few solutions of his own. "Taking the dog for a walk," he wrote. "Cleaning the aquarium." "Cooking." Then he couldn't think of any more.

He slid the curtain to one side and looked out. Nothing but sand, cobblestones, some building debris. He could also see down into the yard of the house next door, which was empty when he went away. Lying on the ground there was now a child's bike with broken handlebars.

A little before half-five he heard the living-room door open and close, followed by his mother's slow footsteps in the hall. Very hesitantly she climbed the stairs. His muscles tensed. She almost never came upstairs. He drew the curtain, grabbed his workbook, leafed through it for a moment and read a few sentences without paying attention. Then the door opened slowly and his mother came in without so much as a word. She sat down on the end of his bed and he quickly put the book back under the pillow.

"It's so lovely to have you back again, son," she said after a while. He could hear her breathing. She smiled and glanced at him. Her gaze slid over to the unfilled aquarium and back to her lap. He didn't know what to say, so he said nothing for a while and then started talking about the bacon and how cheaply he'd been able to pick it up, and about the meal he was going to make. Then he was silent again. Suddenly he felt himself growing terribly tired. Part of him wanted her to stay, to keep sitting there quiet and motionless, but another part wanted her to go away. He knew she'd come to talk.

She kept her hands clasped together on her lap, one thumb over the other. Then she started to fiddle with her necklace. She changed position and stared ahead. With a slow gesture, she wiped some perspiration off her neck.

"You're a sweet boy, Jon," she said, "but you're..." She was searching for words... "You're always so alone."

He didn't say anything in reply, concentrating instead on his breathing. Slowly inhale, hold for a few seconds, exhale. Ten times. What could he say? Should he tell her that she didn't understand him? That he was different from other people? That he didn't need much? She must know that. He looked at her for a second. Her face looked tired. She smiled at him.

"You know what I always say, Jon. People aren't made to be alone so much. We're not animals. People need people."

He didn't know how to respond and kept quiet. Again he wondered exactly what she knew about what had happened.

"Loneliness can do funny things to people, Jon. There's good reasons for the Bible saying we need each other. You were alone too much too. Always occupying yourself with all those animals. That's sweet, but it's not enough." A worried frown passed over her face and her hands drooped down to her lap.

"It is for me," he said, and when she kept looking at him, he averted his eyes. "I'm not like you, Mum."

"I know how you feel about it. You're shy. You prefer being outdoors. But there's more to life."

He noticed her bosom moving every time she gestured with her hands. The necklace with the cross was draped over her collar and trembling slightly to the rhythm of her breathing

"There's something I wanted to tell you," she went on. "The boy who used to live up the street, Herman, you remember, from number seven. Nice lad, but a bit too thirsty." She mimed someone knocking back a glass. "He was always alone too. He started going to weekly Bible meetings in town. He didn't want to at first either, but he's completely perked up. I'll ring up for you, if you like."

The material of her blouse was taut around her breasts. He focused on a sunbeam angling through the room and said, "That's not necessary, Mum." His stomach contracted. She wasn't listening. He wanted to tell her about the therapy, the workbook, the exercise book, the numbers that proved that what he was doing worked and that he was going to make it, but he knew she wouldn't understand. He imagined the way she'd look at him with her eyes screwed up and her mouth pressed tight. She wasn't interested in science. She didn't believe in the power of psychology. And it *was* complicated, he thought. Besides, how could he ever explain what had happened? Or all the things he was working on? What mattered were "coping mechanisms" and "stress regulation", that's what they'd taught him. He didn't fully understand it himself yet either. He felt under his pillow for the exercise book, considering reading a bit to her. But what if she asked questions about it and he couldn't explain?

"With scientific methods, you can investigate them, but religion…" he began, despite knowing better, but she was already talking over him.

"I'll ring up and find out when they have those meetings, just so we know."

They were sitting across from each other, eating from plates with different patterns. His was chipped. It was already half-six, but it was still stifling inside.

"This will be one of the last times we sit in our old kitchen," his mother said. "The letter from the council arrived this week, but I already wrote to tell you that, didn't I? In three weeks we can move in." She smiled. "I'll show you in a bit which house will be ours."

He nodded absently. "How do you like the bacon?"

"Beautiful, son. Nobody fries it up like you do."

Usually they mostly ate fish, which he could bring home cheap from the factory, but the slices of bacon he'd fried smelt so fantastically savoury his mouth was watering. He pushed the point of his knife into the crispy fat, cut, tasted. And again. He was almost ashamed of how hungry he was. But the salty, smoked meat was the most delicious thing he'd tasted in months. His mother smiled at him cautiously, reached for the bottle of wine on the worktop and unscrewed the cap.

"Would you like a glass too? To celebrate being back home together?"

He hesitated for a moment, then shook his head. He wasn't supposed to drink, it weakened your inhibitions. That's what it said in the workbook. It was a "disinhibitor". It could make you impulsive, get you doing things you didn't actually want to do. Fortunately, he didn't even like the sweet white wine she drank. He watched her bosom vibrating slightly while she poured herself a glass, turned away and looked through to the living room in search of Milk. He clicked his tongue. "Where are you, old feller? Come here." The dog came through to the kitchen and stood in front of him wagging his tail. "Here." Jonathan cut off a chunk of bacon and placed it invitingly on the palm of his hand. The dog sat down next to him, sniffed at it with flared, trembling nostrils, licked it a couple of times, then gulped it down in one go.

His mother broke the silence. "Hopefully there'll be a club there where I can play cards. The council's spread the old neighbourhoods out all over town. It'll be a lot of new people living there. I just hope they're not too snooty. I'll never see the old neighbours again."

He nodded. It was his fault. For a second he felt a stabbing pain behind his eyes. If he'd behaved better, she might not have been left here alone all these months. He wondered if she could forgive him.

His mother sighed, took a sip and topped up her glass. He dished up a second helping. In the breaks between her mouthfuls he could heard the tightness of her breathing. She started to cough and kept coughing. Worried, he asked if he should fetch her inhaler, but she said it was all right, took a couple of large gulps of the water he'd poured for her, and calmed down.

"It's the heat, it's so close in here. It's a good thing we're leaving."

He decided not to waste any time before getting boxes from the supermarket to start packing. I'll give myself a week to settle in, a week to pack and a week to clean up. Then they could move.

The next strip of bacon was already impaled on the tines of his fork. He chewed, swallowed and stabbed his fork into a piece of bread, which he dragged through the gravy until it was saturated. It had been a long time since he'd had a decent meal; in prison the food was always bland and overcooked. His stomach was a gaping, apparently unfillable, hole.

"New people have moved in next door, after all," his mother said after a while. "Temporary. It's cheap, of course, a house that's due for demolition." She kept her face bent over her plate. "A mother and a girl."

For a second he thought she was studying him and made sure not to meet her gaze. She stopped eating and rested her

knife and fork on the side of her plate. In the corner of his eye
he saw her looking round the kitchen. He was just about to dip
another piece of bread in the gravy when she resumed talking.
His hand hung over his plate.

"The girl took Milk out for a walk for me every evening. Just
once around the square. Not all the way to the ponds, that's
way too dangerous for a child like that."

He nodded. Under the table he tossed the dog some more
bacon. It sucked it up with a slurping sound.

"Stop it, Jon. Don't feed the dog like that. That girl always used
to bring sausage for him too. I kept on telling her, no feeding."

He smoothed out his hankie and folded it up, then took
another mouthful so he could focus on chewing. Slowly he
ground it all up into a fine paste, his lips clamped shut. Then a
stain in the middle of a flower on the plastic tablecloth caught
his eye. He spat on his fingers and started to rub.

"Now you're here, that won't be necessary any more, thank
goodness. You can just take Milk out for a walk yourself."

Often it was like her words were forcing their way into his
head via secret routes and slowly building up the pressure. He
took his hankie and wiped his throat with his eyes closed.

His mother put down her fork and breathed out before
saying, "The mother's working in that new bar, Storm, down at
the harbour. She leaves that girl to fend for herself. It's hard to
fathom, a woman in her position leaving her child alone all day."

He'd picked a sponge up off the worktop and started his
meticulous wiping of the tablecloth. His mother sipped her
wine and he heard her sniff a couple of times. Suddenly, he
was overcome by exhaustion and felt a pain in his back. And,
to his own annoyance, this time it was her silence he couldn't
bear. For a moment he had the impression she knew more than
he thought she knew and that was possibly the reason she'd

consented so readily to not coming to visit him, but he refused
to give in to the feelings that brought. Instead he asked if she
was finished with her plate. Sitting at the table together made
him too nervous. He quickly stacked the plates and pans, filled
the sink and put a pan of milk on the stove while waiting for
the water to drip through the coffee filter.

"Shall I bring the coffee through to the living room, Mum?"

"Lovely, son," she said. "Nice." She struggled up onto her feet.

After doing the washing-up, he beat the dust out of the blanket
they used as a cover for the sofa, mopped the kitchen floor and
aired his mother's bedroom. He used the narrow nozzle of
the vacuum cleaner to get down into the cracks between the
living-room floorboards and sucked up the accumulated dust.
Then he withdrew to his room to do another exercise. He'd
worked out that if he did two a day, he'd have the workbook
completed in exactly three weeks. By the time they moved
he'd be back to his old self and as strong as ever. He'd have
been through it all and could start again at the first exercise.
Repetition was important, according to the psychologist. He'd
also said that some people learn more easily than others.
Everyone retains information in their own way: some by reading, some by doing.

"For you, Jonathan, repetition is important, a lot of repetition." The psychologist had explained something about his
short-term memory. "But you're very good at remembering
details for a long time." He'd explained that to get the total
overview he had to do things over and over again. That wasn't
a problem. Jonathan liked writing these things down and that
was to his advantage. He could reread it all whenever he liked.
He imagined it as the needle of the old-fashioned record player

his mother still had in the cupboard. Every time he played that same record, the grooves would get deeper.

There were still annoying stripes of sunlight on the wall. He closed the curtains, but because they didn't meet properly, even after he'd pegged them together, light still glared through the gaps. He'd have to ignore it.

He sat down at his table, took his workbook from the bed, opened it, raised his pen and looked down at his hands. He glanced at the clock, which was ticking softly. Twenty-eight minutes past seven; he'd start at seven thirty. Downstairs he heard his mother turn a tap on and then off while singing a sad-sounding song. She was singing to the dog through the TV buzz.

He read the assignment. "Your solutions," it said at the top. "Protective factors." That was what it was about. He read the page quietly to himself.

He thought about it for a while, then stood up, walked over to his bed, sat down on it for a second, stood up again and went over to the window. He opened it and looked down at the neighbour's yard. It was quiet outside. Just bare paving stones, the child's bike. Now there was a big orange space hopper next to it. Not a single noise from inside the house.

He thought about the fish he'd seen swimming over the bottom of the pond this afternoon. They'd been so beautiful in their simplicity. A human could never be that perfect. A muscle in the corner of his eye started to vibrate. He sniffed and forced his eyes back to his assignment: an overview of how he could structure his life in the period ahead.

The window was still open and noises from further afield were drifting into his room. A ship's horn, the screech of a gull. "Work and free time," it said. "Daily schedule and structure." Structure: he knew that was an important word. He started with his daily schedule, writing it in pencil first with his rubber ready for action. Behind him the fan was on. It was still hot. A drop of sweat fell from his forehead onto the page. He used a hankie he'd just got out of his wardrobe drawer to carefully soak it up. Then he wrote down his schedule, with short interruptions now and then to wipe the sweat from his face. His mumbling lips formed the words. He kept writing until he'd filled the whole day, hour by hour. Then he started to trace the words in pen. He managed to stay calm. He wrote:

Get up at 5 a.m.
Walk Milk at 5.30 a.m.
The 6.30 a.m. to 2.30 p.m. shift at Pronk Fish
    Processing
3 p.m.: walk Milk second time. Ask my mother if she
    can let him out in the yard in between times.
From 3.30 to 5.30 p.m.: clean the house, help my
    mother
From 5.30 to 6 p.m.: do first assignment
From 6 to 6.30 p.m.: cook
6.30 p.m.: eat
From 7.30 to 8 p.m.: do second assignment
8 p.m.: walk Milk third time
8.30 to 10 p.m.: drink coffee with my mother.

When he had time, he thought, he could play a game of cards with her. And go through the two assignments again. He wrote that down too.

10.00 p.m.: go to bed.

He decided against making a separate daily schedule for the weekend.

When he was finished he stood up, crossed the room and stared into the empty glass tank. He sat down again. "Space for notes and your own thoughts," he read. He thought about it, took the cap off his pen and wrote "Better," below the heading. "I'll get better." That was all he could think of. He underlined it and added a series of exclamation marks.

After that he waited for a while to see if he had any more thoughts of his own. He gazed pensively at the paper. The sound of the TV reached him through the floor. He tried to encourage himself: "You can do it." And: "You're a hard worker, Jon." But every time he thought of something, it blurred again in the noise from downstairs. The television, his mother, the dog's barking and whimpering. He'd forgotten how noisy it was here. His thoughts all seemed silly anyway, too trivial to remember.

He needed some earplugs, he thought. And it was almost time for Milk's walk. He went into the bathroom and opened the medicine cabinet. Between the toiletries and the make-up his mother had long stopped using, he found a remnant of a packet of cotton wool. He picked some off, rolled it into a small hard ball between his fingers and popped it into his mouth to wet it. A few threads came loose. He sucked on the ball to turn it into a smooth plug he could push into his ear, then made another.

Just when he'd sat down again, the doorbell rang. And then a second time straight away. He sighed and pulled the plugs out of his ears. Who could that be? The neighbourhood was empty. Through the sound of the TV, he heard his mother shuffling out of the living room and opening the hall door.

He dried his sweaty palms on his jeans and walked to the window. The space hopper was gone. In the roof gutter a pigeon was having a bath in a grimy puddle, its feet scratching over the zinc. A small feather that could come loose at any moment was stuck to the tip of its right wing. Suddenly he saw that the neighbours' back door was open. Quietly he crept out onto the landing.

"I thought you already knew you didn't have to come any more?" He could tell from her voice that his mother wasn't at her ease.

"Can I take Milk out for one more walk?" The other voice seemed to come from further away.

"No, sweetie, my son's back home now. You don't need to any more. I've already told you that so many times."

He stood motionless on the top step for a few seconds. Then moved closer.

"Couldn't we do it together?" he heard the girl ask. "Or take turns?"

He checked his breathing—inhale slowly, slowly exhale—went down the last steps and pushed open the hall door.

"There he is. My son," his mother said, glancing at him in passing.

The child was standing at least half a metre back from the doorstep. She looked up at him shyly through a lock of hair that had fallen down in front of her eyes. "Hi, I'm Elke." She pushed her lower lip out a little and tried to blow the hair out of the way. It immediately flopped back down in the same place.

"Hurry up now, Jon," his mother said through the hall door, "it's high time." He could hear the dog somewhere behind him.

His mother walked off, looking back a couple of times over her shoulder. The girl stayed where she was. She was trying to look past him, searching for the dog, of course, he thought. Meanwhile his mother's footsteps moved further down the hall. He heard her coughing in the kitchen. "Come on, hurry up, you. Outside," she growled at the dog.

The child was still standing there.

He kept his head down, but studied her through his lashes.

She was small, only up to his chest. Dressed in a faded top and cheap flip-flops. Her blonde hair was pulled back into a short ponytail held together with an elastic hairband. It wasn't actually long enough to tie back properly and a lank lock was hanging down the side of her face. She scratched at a graze on her elbow.

She studied him carefully. "Are you going to take Milk out for his walks now?" She was pouting a little.

"Yes. Yeah. From now on I'll be walking him again." He hoped his voice sounded as determined as he'd intended.

The girl took another step back but stayed there on the pavement, slowly wobbling from one foot to the other. They stood opposite each other without speaking. He tried to look past her but his eyes were drawn towards her. Somehow he felt compelled to look at her again.

She was very young, he thought, not ten yet. He could still see a little down on her throat. She had small, sweet, endearing ears. Don't, he thought. Don't think like that. Before you know it, you'll have thoughts that aren't good. Cognitive distortions. Or justifications. Or something else. For the moment he didn't know what exactly, but he'd look it up.

Just when he was about to call him, Milk came shuffling out of the hall and appeared by his side. Maybe he'd recognized the girl's voice, because he went up to her with his tail wagging. She grabbed the dog's head with both hands—"Milky!"—knelt down and wrapped her arms around his neck, whispering things in his ear that visibly calmed him. Milk sank to the ground and, growling softly, pushed his muzzle against her cheek. The girl got down even lower, stretched out and began patting him all over. With her fingers curled, she scratched his coat quickly, hurriedly, just like Jonathan always did.

A lot of people found Milk disgusting. He was old and scrawny, with chafed spots on his sides. After you'd touched him, your fingertips smelt like him and gleamed from the greasy film on his coat. Even Betsy from the flats hadn't wanted to touch him. "Yuck," she'd say, shaking her head slightly. "He's dirty, he needs a bath."

Despite his best intentions his eyes followed her fingers over the folds of skin around the dog's head. Milk's eyes were closed. Then Jonathan noticed her nails. They were chewed and neglected. He still found it endearing.

"I know exactly what he likes," she said. "Look. You have to rub his ears like this, and then, what's it called, like this around his neck. Look. Here. Like this." And again he watched her two hands at work. She had her chin raised slightly and kept her eyes fixed on Jonathan's face, while her fingers went over Milk's wiry coat once again.

He needed to walk away, he knew that, but he stayed put. This is the practice, he thought, trying to remember a sentence he'd read in the introduction to the workbook. The interventions were investigated with a follow-up period six months after treatment and, how did it go again, they measured the percentages after six months too—he wasn't sure of the exact figures, but they were promising. Or did they use a different word? He shouldn't dwell on it.

"Here, boy," he said, interrupting his own train of thought. "We're going."

She looked up at him for a moment with a frown, then resumed talking, ignoring what he'd just said. "He's not very good-looking, but he's the sweetest animal I know. We get on really well." She stayed where she was, patting Milk and talking to him in a low voice. She wiped the hair out of her eyes again with the back of her hand and again it fell back down. "And

I know everything about animals. Do you want to see what I can do with him?" She fell silent and looked up expectantly. She seemed to be hoping for his approval.

He really wanted to leave now, but still stayed there with his hands clenched tightly in his pockets. And the child stayed where she was too, as if gathering her courage. She held her fingertips in front of the dog's snout. Milk stretched out his scrawny neck and gave them a good sniff. Then she moved her face so close to the dog's open mouth that she could surely feel his rank breath blowing out over it. She shot him a look of triumph. "Are you brave enough to do that?"

He listened to the dog's soft panting and stared at her lips, which were slightly parted. Her teeth were showing. They were a little too big for her mouth. When she gave a cautious smile, slightly crooked, he noticed that a piece of her right front tooth was broken off, a chip. He couldn't take his eyes off it. He automatically ran his tongue over his own front teeth. She saw the look in his eyes. "What happened to your front tooth?" He'd already said the words. He nodded quickly at her mouth.

She let go of the dog and stood up. She deliberately pushed her lower lip forward, sniffed and frowned, as if it was something she needed to think deeply about. Her knees were turned slightly inward. "Nothing special." She looked up at the sky for a second, then added, "Fell over." She shrugged as if racking her brain even more and wondering how exactly it had happened. "I slipped at the swimming pool."

He looked over the top of her head at the expanse of bare sand. A breeze had come up and was now pushing at a light branch on the ground. With short teasing nudges it began to roll it along ahead of it.

He was overcome by a vague sense of tension. The warning-sign chart lit up in his head. "Phase one: you are relaxed." Was he relaxed? No, he thought, but he never was really. Did that mean that this was already phase two? That couldn't be right either. That was when he was thinking the wrong things, and what else was it? The wrong thoughts, anyway. And he wasn't having them. Later, after Milk's walk, he'd go through the chart again. The main thing now was to get away as fast as possible, before his head got even fuller.

"Come on, boy." He gave Milk's collar a cautious tug, but the dog didn't budge.

The girl scratched her right calf with the partly detached trim of her other flip-flop. "It was at the swimming lesson," she continued. "When I fell over. And then I was too scared to swim any more."

He clipped the leash onto the collar. He felt like she was coming closer. "Nasty. Well, we have to get going."

He thought of his mother, looked back for a moment but couldn't see her. "Come on, Milk," he said as brightly as he could. "Come on."

"I was the only one in the class without a badge," she said. While studying him through her hair, she plucked at the material of her top with her thumb and index finger. It had an embroidered flower on it. He saw that there was a light glow floating in her right eye, a copper-coloured stain that covered part of the iris, as if her two eyes were each a different colour. It gave her an air of mystery. He looked away from it at once, as if someone had jerked his head back from behind.

"Come on, boy," he repeated, pulling the leash.

She started talking again. "I'm going to learn how to swim, really. I'm not stupid, in case you think so. Or do you not believe me? I was actually allowed to skip a year. I was in a, what's it called, a special class, but when Dad still lived with us, he didn't want that. At my new school, after the holidays, I'm going to get all my badges. Bronze, silver and gold. In a really big swimming pool, because we're going to have to move again. We're not allowed to stay here too long, but I'm not allowed to talk about that. Mum's working really hard to make enough money. Then we're leaving."

He nodded, not really listening. He wanted to hear what she had to say, but at the same time he didn't. Her voice was lovely, a soft murmur. Meanwhile he looked at the sun and realized it was getting late. If he wasn't careful, things would start to slip. He had to keep a tight schedule. He heard her saying something about her mother's job.

"A really stupid job at that bar; she works all day. The only people who go there are men who drink way too much, and then they just sit there staring at her boobs."

He was shocked. But couldn't stop his gaze from descending to hers, which were still flat. He could very vaguely make out the shadow of her breastbone through the material. Ashamed of himself, he looked away, pulled back his shoulders, breathed in and out deeply and cleared his throat. Then he took a step past her, pulling the dog along behind him.

"Where are you going?" she asked.

"The dunes." He'd wanted to stick to a small circuit of the empty neighbourhood, but that wasn't possible now. This made it easier to shake her off. He gave a half-hearted nod in the direction of the dunes.

"Can I come?"

"No. From now on, I'll be taking Milk out for his walks again. Alone." He gave another tug on the leash. When Milk ignored him again, he bent over, patted the loose skin behind his ears and pulled gently on the leash. Finally, the dog got up.

With the uncomfortable heat on his neck, he walked off. He thought about moving and everything he had to do. He'd make a list, a timeline. Get some boxes, do the dusting, sort things out, pack, write the change-of-address cards.

Just when he'd built up a retaining wall of his own thoughts inside his head, he heard her voice a few steps behind him. "Do you know what my mum said?" Her voice was louder now. He turned. She had her eyes screwed up and he couldn't place her expression. "My mum says I can play anywhere I like as long as I don't come here."

Suddenly he stopped. Without wanting to, he stared at her. She was holding her head at an angle and looking at him through her hair. She blew it out of her eyes and it fell back down again. She was studying him carefully. "She says you're not nice at all."

"Come on, Milk," he urged. "Get a move on." The back of his neck was now burning so badly it felt like the little hairs were being scorched. He looked around one last time. She was pushing the tuft of hair back behind her ear.

Later that evening he stood at his bedroom window. It was still so hot it was almost unbearable. In the distance the sun was setting behind the roofs. He cautiously touched the skin of his face. His cheeks, his stubble, his chin, the scar over his lip. I *am* good, he thought, and repeated it, quietly whispering to himself, *I am good*. He tried to remember the sentences from the introduction he'd discussed with the psychologist and read in the workbook yesterday. He squeezed his eyes shut, searching his memory. Eventually they came back to him. "It's not about me," he said out loud. "It's not about me, but about my actions, about…" He hesitated. "It's just my behaviour."

He stepped over to his table, picked up the book, sat down on the bed and leafed through it until he found the passage. "In this therapy we discuss offences and behaviour that are trans-gressive." Oh, yeah, that was it. He went back to the window. "It is our actions and offences that are transgressive," he said quietly to the window, in which he could see his own vague reflection. "We learn to control that behaviour." He read on, repeating the last sentences over and over again: "The offender is not bad as a person; it is the acts that are transgressive. Here we learn how to control those acts."

AFTER WAKING UP, Jonathan lay motionless in bed for a while. He clamped his eyes shut and raised a hand to his forehead to block out the light that was already streaming in. It was quarter past six, as he'd just seen on his alarm clock. Sunday. Lukewarm air was drifting into the room through the open window and gently rippling the curtain. He sighed, tired from the long day yesterday. But he still got up and walked to the small bathroom attached to his room. I have to go to bed earlier, he thought while washing at the sink. Real life has started. Things are tiring. The heat gets to you.

At exactly half past, he started on his first circuit with Milk. The sun had only been up for an hour and the light in the streets was still pale, but it was already warm.

He'd heard his mother doing rounds of the yard in her slippers earlier in the morning. He knew that she sometimes went outside at the crack of dawn to try to get more air. I have to help her, he thought, and again it felt like everything was his fault. The heat, the shabby house, the equally humble home they would soon be moving into.

He shook off the thought with all his strength, like a dog driving raindrops out of its coat. In the kitchen he made a large jug of squash with ice cubes, which clicked quietly against each other as he carried them outside. His mother had sat down on the bench against the back wall, her face in the shade from the house. While she drank, he set to work. He shook out her sheets, hoovered the dust particles out of her mattress, wiped the surfaces in the living room and bedroom down with a wet sponge, made some sandwiches and fed the dog. Then he took her the pack of cards. It was nine o'clock.

But before he'd let himself go to the dunes, he had to sit down at his table for a while; he did a thought-stopping exercise and repeated his daily schedule out loud to himself a few times in an attempt to learn it off by heart.

Now and then he stood up to look through the split in the curtains at the house next door. He wondered where the girl was. But he kept forcing himself to concentrate on the task at hand. He pictured the psychologist's face before him while he was doing it. As if they were once again sitting opposite each other at his big desk. The way the man relaxed with one elbow on the desktop and his other hand resting on Jonathan's dossier. He also saw the muscles in his big, broad jaw tensing and his pupils contracting a little while he listened or waited for Jonathan to answer one of his questions.

"Today I'd like to discuss the results of the psychological evaluation with you, Jonathan." Always that look he found so hard to interpret. A verbal flood followed. Numbers, numbers, numbers. In no time his head was spinning. The psychologist told him his IQ, having already explained all kinds of things about it. But no matter how attentively Jonathan had listened, he'd already forgotten most of it. His score was lower than average, that much he remembered; it wasn't nice to hear. But it turned out there were other things he could do very well, better than other people. Doing a neat job, being diligent and persistent, concentrating for a long time on one subject.

He was also given a rating on a scale for psychopaths: that was low, but there were other reasons why the therapists thought there was a significant chance of his doing something like it again. It was only because the prosecutor hadn't been able to get the evidence together and he couldn't be convicted on the victim's statement alone, his lawyer had explained. Otherwise he would not just have a sentence still to serve, but also be under a hospital order.

"We estimate a high likelihood of a repeat offence with crimes like yours." Jonathan fitted a profile, the psychologist had explained, an offender profile, and he'd quoted percentages that had washed out of Jonathan's brain as fast as he'd heard them. They'd only left vague traces, shallow gullies, bird prints in the sand.

In his cell at night he'd lain on his bed and stared at the ceiling. He ran his hands over his body, rubbing his chest, throat and face. Even though he knew it was nonsense he was looking for something under his skin, a thickening, a hollow, something that explained the percentages in that profile. Something that matched the things he'd heard that day. Was that really him? It was a frightening yet reassuring idea that the experts seemed to know him better than he knew himself.

That hospital order could last a long time, the psychologist had told him; he had to take that into account. It could be followed by a restriction order. That was why it was so important for him to apply himself as best he could now. There were still no guarantees of quick results, and the treatment could be extended every year, theoretically for ever, until the psychiatrists and psychologists at the hospital judged him to be cured.

A hospital order—he'd seen folders from that hospital. Twelve men on a ward, thin-walled cells on either side of a narrow corridor. It would be too much for him. He wouldn't be able to bear the constant proximity of the others. Year in, year out, their smells, their noise, their bodies. As soon as the other men found out what he was in for, they'd get him, that was inevitable. One way or another, he wouldn't come out alive. He sighed. As horrific as that hospital order had seemed, he would have liked to have carried on longer with the pre-therapy with the prison psychologist. But that was all cancelled once he was acquitted. Now he could only sign up voluntarily. There was a centre in the city. The psychologist had given him the telephone number, but he knew it was a step he would never dare take.

Towards ten he pulled his waders on in the utility room and went back outside. He crossed the yard to the shed, which served as a storage room. It was less than five paces across and gave off a permanent, vague smell of mould. Old newspapers covered the floor. A lot of the windowpanes were broken and shards of glass were sticking up out of the putty like razor-sharp fangs. It was horrible. He could hardly bear the sight of it and had been planning on getting it fixed up for years. There was just never any money. And now the house was going to be demolished and it was too late.

In the semi-darkness he patted the wall until he found the switch. The bulb on the ceiling flicked on. Fine dust floated through the light.

This was where he'd hidden that afternoon. The afternoon he was going to be arrested. He knew what was going to happen, that there was no point in hiding. But he still hid behind a few crates containing old pumps he'd been meaning to fix. There was a stabbing pain behind his eyes. Betsy and he had even walked back home together side by side, silent, her head trembling even more intensely than usual. "Don't tell your mum, OK?" he'd said. "Our little secret." Such a coward. He'd hated himself for it.

He held his breath for a moment and listened to the silence surrounding him. All those thoughts he had, from now on he'd turn them round. "You *have* thoughts"—he repeated what he'd read in the workbook—"but your thoughts are *not* you."

In the dim light of the bulb he studied the rods that were hanging here, tidily, from small to large, on the brick wall. The only one that didn't really belong in the series was the bamboo rod he'd made as a child. He just couldn't bring himself to throw it away.

He wanted to catch something big today and chose a light feeder and a casting rod. For hooks he chose a blue Aberdeen 8 and a 10: razor sharp, very strong and thin. He threaded a line through the rods and leant them against the wall, ready to rest them on his shoulder. He wanted to take the binoculars too, the hand net and the bucket.

Then he walked across the yard and back into the kitchen to get the bait ready. If he wanted to catch a big, strong perch or rudd, good bait was essential. He put on some water, peeled three potatoes, boiled them and cut them up into equal cubes, opened a tin of sweetcorn, shook the square grains out into a container and sweetened them with some sugar. Then he cut off a piece of cheese and took some of Milk's dry food with him. He got his rucksack from upstairs and stacked all the bait containers into it. Finally, he collected the rods, bucket and floats and he was ready to go.

The sky was light and dazzling. It was warming up fast. His mother stood near the back door in her housecoat, fanning herself with her Bible. She squinted out at the heat, anxiously studying the high, cloudless, already quivering sky. Each time she took a puff from her inhaler, there was a brief, dry rattling sound. She pointed up. "It's going to be a stinker today."

"I'm only staying until I catch something good. For my aquarium, maybe something good to eat."

"That'd be nice."

It was quiet for a moment, but he felt there was something else she wanted to say. He held his tongue, fiddling with the rods.

"What are you after out there?" she asked eventually. Her voice didn't sound annoyed, like he'd feared. And again. "What on earth do you do there all the time? All by yourself at those deserted little lakes?"

He coughed and let his breath escape through his nostrils. The arteries in his forehead were throbbing from the heat. Meanwhile he thought about all those indescribably quiet afternoons he'd spent out there alone, how happy he'd been. He couldn't explain to her how everything out there was frozen even when it was moving. Time didn't exist. There wasn't any past or future. The only thing he needed to do was breathe in and out, sit and watch. Nobody wanted anything from him.

"I'm just going fishing, like always. That's what I do there. I fish. Alone."

"In a couple of hours you won't be able to stand it out in the dunes." She tapped the back of her inhaler, raised it to her lips, but lowered it again.

He thought of what she always said about life being an ordeal. Maybe this was her ordeal. Always being stuck at home without having anywhere she could go to be at peace, like him.

She stood there appraising his face.

"A nice day's fishing," he said. "Tomorrow back at work. And who knows what I'll catch. Maybe I can fry up a pike-perch for you for tea."

This seemed to please her, because he saw that she was now smiling at him. "You're a funny feller. Just be careful, OK?"

"Of course."

He whistled the dog, who was stretched out in the shade of the shed. He had to do it a couple of times, but then Milk came shuffling over with his stiff-legged gait. Jonathan patted him on the head for a moment, then attached his leash.

Just before he left, the girl's face popped into his thoughts. The look in those peculiar eyes. There was something sad about her. But he still found her inexpressibly beautiful. He quickly suppressed the thought, getting rid of it as fast as it had appeared.

Moving warily, he took the dirt road, which had clumps of grass growing in it here and there, keeping his eyes fixed on the ground. After a few metres he hesitated, stopped and looked over his shoulder. The girl was playing with a ball in the distance. Immediately he turned and carried on.

With the old dog limping along behind him, he headed west along the edge of the village. Now too there was nobody around. By the time they reached the dunes Milk had fallen behind. Jonathan slowed down and waited until the dog had passed him and was walking in front, with his head down, his quivering snout pointing at the ground. The sun rose quickly, spreading relentless heat. Getting closer to the ponds, Jonathan kept looking up and peering at the sky. Sometimes he felt lost for a moment, as if he was dissolving in that emptiness. But he stopped the feeling in its tracks.

He took the northernmost, shortest path to the ponds. It was covered with shells that crunched under his feet. The sun was burning the top of his head. At the old sandpit he pushed through the reeds and cut some with his pocketknife to clear a spot where he could sit with the dog. He called him with a short whistle; Milk stood still for a moment, unsure of what was expected of him. Then, with his eyes squeezed shut, he pushed his trembling snout out towards the water and ambled over. He lay down by the waterside, crossed his front paws and dozed off. Jonathan gave him a good scratch on the head and wiped some gunk out of his eye with a corner of his hankie. A cloudy film had formed over his eyes in his old age. "There you go, buddy." He put some dry dog food in the feeder and attached it to the biggest float. Every few minutes he wiped the sweat from his brow.

When he still hadn't caught anything after a couple of hours, he broke a branch off a bush and poked around in the mud and sludge, dredging up a handful of water snails, bithynia, which he put in a jar with some water. They floated in slow circles, occasionally brushing the glass with their tails.

He resumed his position next to his casting rod and sat there waiting. No longer directly overhead, the sun had begun its descent to the west, but there was still no sign of the day beginning to cool off.

The trees on the far side of the lake seemed to be moving in the shimmering air. He poured some water into his cupped hand to give the dog a drink, then took a slug from the bottle himself. He'd replaced the dog food with sweetcorn, but when he still hadn't had a bite an hour later, he changed back to dog food and then cheese. Now and then he saw the shadows he'd seen yesterday gliding over the bottom, but for a long time absolutely nothing happened. He still stared at the water and his float the whole time. Images of the girl from next door flashed through his mind now and then. Her broken tooth, the lock of hair falling over her forehead, her ear. And then he quickly refocused on the ripples in the water.

It got even hotter. He threaded a snail onto his hook. Cast it out and waited. His back was itching from the heat. He pulled off his T-shirt and let the sun burn his skin until he couldn't bear it, gathered up his things and fled to the shade of the pine

Milk had already sought out and fallen asleep under. After a while he went back to the water's edge.

With every sigh of wind the reeds behind him rustled. He looked back a couple of times but there was nothing to see. Once a jackdaw landed on a branch of the hawthorn, looked out past him for a while, spread its wings and flew off.

He put out the feeder with a lump of bait and waited. Now and then he had a bite. With quick movements he pulled up the line and enjoyed the splashing water sparkling in the light. A few times he pulled in small, wriggling fish, common bream, one silver bream, looking at them briefly but carefully in the sunlight, studying the curve of the line from their gills to their tail, their small eyes.

Towards three one of the big shadows came floating up from the depths. Immediately Jonathan sat up straight and crept forward, making sure not to move the rod in the water. He saw a powerful silhouette with a broad head. It swam slowly around the bait without biting. Waiting.

Jonathan bent forward and peered into the water through the shadow of his own face. Slow and cautious, the fish circled. For a while it stayed still next to the float, its tail moving calmly. Its beautiful arched back glowing red in the sun's rays. What was it? A carp, after all?

"Show yourself, boy," he whispered. "I won't hurt you."

The fish was still hardly moving, just its tail swinging softly from side to side, and otherwise suspended motionless in the water.

"Come on, don't be scared."

He was starting to worry about the fish. It seemed so lethargic. I can make you better, he thought. You're going to die here. He bent further forward, sliding on his knees until he was as close to the edge as he could get, then stuck his hands into the water. He spread his fingers and fluttered his hands, before lying on his stomach and sliding forward and down towards the fish, hanging over the water, so close he could almost touch it. All this time the fish stayed still in the water, gently moving its tail. Then all at once it sank down into the depths, was gone for a moment, then appeared again even closer to the bank.

Jonathan quickly backed up from the bank, crept over to the shaded spot where he'd left his fishing gear and grabbed his net. Once again he lay down on his stomach on the side of the pond. And waited. Cautiously he inched the net closer to the fish, which kept swimming away from him, before coming back again. Finally, he felt it was the right moment. He tensed his back, managed to get the net under the fish's body in one smooth movement and pulled it up and out.

He could hardly believe it. He'd got him. The fish twisted and wriggled for a moment, but then lay big and still in the net, gleaming in the afternoon sun, its head and back golden red. A tench. He recognized it immediately. The round fins, orange-red eyes, tiny, deep scales and thick paintbrush tail. Tench didn't do well in the heat, he knew that; maybe that was why this one was so weak.

"Haven't you been able to hunt, boy?" he asked, slowly lifting the net out of the water. "Are you hungry?" He saw that it had a nasty gash on its belly. From a bird, he thought, probably a cormorant or a large gull.

"Does that hurt? Something got you there." With me you'll never have to be hungry again, he thought.

The dog yapped around his legs excitedly. "Not now, Milk." Ruffling his coat with one hand, he managed to calm him down and went back to talking to the fish, softly, admiring it while he was at it. It was a male. He could tell from the large pelvic fins with the thick outer ray. And perfectly clean. No tubercles and the skin, so often slimy with tench, nice and smooth. He held the heavy fish in his arms. To his surprise he felt his tear ducts filling. He sniffed and swallowed.

Wanting to get home as fast as possible, he bundled up his things and headed off. Trotting through the dunes, along the alleys and narrow streets behind the harbour, the fish in the bucket. He tried to walk tall with his chest out, proud of his catch, but his shoulders drooped and the tension in his neck and back increased, as if he was expecting a blow to land any moment.

Meanwhile his eyes were screwed almost shut against the light. It was so hot now it was like fine, white dust falling on the village.

His heart pounded in his chest. A tench. Or a "doctor fish". That was what they used to call them, he didn't remember why, but he'd read it somewhere. He'd look it up later in his nature encyclopaedia. Doctor fish. A nice name. He repeated it a few times under his breath while giving little tugs on the leash to keep the worn-out dog moving. Thinking about the tench and the prospect of its quiet company every day from now on, company he wouldn't have to share with anyone, he started walking faster. I'll make sure you get your strength back, he thought. He would keep this big strong fish with him for a long time.

He encountered the girl just a few metres from his house. She was alone, playing in the sand. He saw right away that she was wearing the same clothes as the day before: the running shorts with stitching that had once been white, the crumpled top with a flower on it. She was bent over to draw, her space hopper behind her, tracing shapes in the dust with her fingers. Every now and then some whirled up. There was an exercise book next to her on the pavement. She must have been concentrating hard because she didn't seem to hear him.

He wavered for a moment, resisting the temptation to whisper her name, Elke, so that she would turn around and he could show her the fish. Don't do it, he thought. This is what the psychologist would call an impulse. Something you do without thinking. Think things through.

His hands tightened around the handle of the bucket. Tension spread through his fingers and settled in his knuckles. He looked at her neck, the shadow of her back. He could see the outline of her shoulder blades under her top. I should walk away. In his thoughts he turned on his heel and strode off in the other direction. But before he could move, the dog started barking. Too late.

The child jumped up, rushed over to the dog and bent over him. Elated, he put his paws on her thighs so she could pat him. When she squatted, he moved even closer and sat to give her face a good licking. She giggled. "Hey, Milk," he heard her saying, "you gonna come and play with me? You coming?" The dog gave a short bark. "Come and play with me, 'cause it's so *boooring* here." She sniffed. "My mother has to work all the time and I miss you."

He now noticed that she spoke with a slight lisp, as if her tongue was making little bubbles of spit against the back of her teeth. He looked at her from the corner of his eye. Her nostrils were trembling. Her cheek was lit from the side by the afternoon sun and only now could he see properly how soft her skin was—her throat seemed even more delicate than yesterday. Just stay there, he said to her in his thoughts. Not too close. Just to be sure he shuffled a little with his feet, taking an almost imperceptible step away.

The girl was mumbling compliments to the dog, whose whole body was panting in the heat. Although the sun was already low, it was still murderously hot.

He turned his gaze to the graze on her elbow. It was half covered with a scab but quite large. Why hadn't her mother put a plaster on it? Or she herself? He couldn't look at it for too long, it made him feel a bit queasy. For a moment he felt an urge to do something about it, to go inside to get a piece of gauze, a bandage, to clean the wound with iodine or alcohol.

At the edge of his thoughts he suddenly heard her talking. "What's that?" she asked. She came closer and looked into the bucket. "Hey, I asked you a question—you listening?"

"I just caught it in the dunes."

I can see you're alone, he said to himself, imagining how the conversation could go. I can dress your wound and you can help me with the dog and... He didn't complete the thought. Everything that popped into his mind was now immediately crossed out by the workbook words that came bubbling up. He needed to avoid high-risk situations, that was one of the most important points. And then you had coping mechanisms, ways of dealing with stress. Looking for distractions, hobbies, trying to get your problems out of your system by writing them down. He had to keep scoring high on all those fronts. He nibbled the inside of his cheek.

"What a beautiful fish—is that a carp?" she asked. She had come up next to him and was bending over the bucket. A very faint smell of perspiration rose up to meet him.

"No, not a carp." He was surprised she even knew what a carp looked like.

As if she could read his mind, she added, "I told you I know all about animals." Again she held her head at a slight angle and gave him a cautious smile. He saw her damaged tooth.

"It's a tench," he said, "a very special fish. It's part of the carp family, but a different species. It's easy to tell it's not a carp from the tail, see?" He almost started another sentence but thought better of it. He'd said too much already. Just like yesterday. Somehow he talked more than he wanted to when he was with her; she drew the words out of him and he stayed there against his wishes. He squeezed his lips together. It just kept getting hotter. All the way to the horizon the sky was full of white clouds, dense and low. Now and then a gust of wind brought the smell of the harbour. A vague mix of salt and fuel oil.

"It's enormous," she blurted, hopping excitedly from one foot to the other. He looked at her space hopper. "It's so big, it looks like a pike. Sometimes I used to go fishing with our old neighbour, before, and once we caught a, what's it called, a grass carp."

"Really?"

He swallowed, anxious to escape the conversation. Her words had threaded together into a net that had been tossed over him and could draw tighter at any moment.

"Is that your favourite animal," she asked, "those fish? Mine's horses." Those eyes again, looking straight into his. "Or dogs," she continued, frowning, as if she had to think hard about what to choose. "I had a dog for a while once too, but not very long, and then she died. It was really sad."

"I like all animals," he said. "But I have to get this one into some cold water soon because otherwise it's going to get too hot."

"Yes, that would be sad. If the weather gets too hot, maybe it'd get sick. And if the weather gets super-hot, people get sick too, don't they? Sometimes, if they're old, they even die," she said without taking a breath. "I saw it on the news."

"Yes, that can be very dangerous. I'm going inside now." He looked away, but when he looked back he saw that she was standing there with her feet turned in again, as cute as yesterday. He glanced at her tooth. She smiled, but there was something in her eyes that made him feel uncomfortable. Maybe he'd disappointed her by wanting to go away already, maybe she was feeling lonely. He didn't want to think about it.

At home he wanted to go straight upstairs so he could quickly let the fish glide into the water and be alone again. It was all too much. Too many impressions, too many unexpected events. He imagined himself lying stretched out on the floor next to the aquarium, his T-shirt off, the window open, the fan turned on. He longed to hear nothing but the water pump and the pigeon's feet, feeling the air on his sweaty body.

But his mother must have already heard or seen him, because when he went inside she emerged from the living room to meet him in the hall. He wondered if she'd already started on the wine. He'd seen the cards on the sofa through the window. She'd been playing patience all afternoon, of course, mumbling the scores to herself, counting them on her fingers, TV cackling in the background.

She came closer. To his relief he saw the glint he knew so well in her eye. A sign she was in a good mood. She wouldn't be too hard on him. "So," she said, "has my boy had a nice day today?"

He hadn't had a chance to formulate an answer before her eyes had latched onto the bucket he was holding. She came a little closer and bent over. "Good heavens, Mother of God, what have you got now?" Her forehead puckered up in horror.

He curled his fingers tighter around the handle of the bucket. "It's a tench." He wondered what to do. He'd seen on the church clock that it had already gone four. Getting the fish set up properly would take a couple of hours, he wanted to rest, Milk would need walking again later, he still had to hoover. A force inside him, or maybe outside, was pursuing him, casting its shadow over him and making him feel like something ominous would happen if he left a single minute unfilled. It pressed against his knees from behind, for a moment it was like his legs were going to buckle, his breath was taut, he had to go on. But an irresistible flood of words was also rising up inside him.

"It's a tench," he began again, explaining that it was a member of the carp family but not a real carp. "It's a very special fish. They used to call it a doctor fish too."

"A doctor fish," he heard his mother repeating quietly. "What a strange name." She bent closer to get a better idea of the length of the fish. "It's enormous."

He kept talking about the characteristics of tench, what he could remember at least, but soon noticed that her thoughts were already wandering. He stopped talking, sniffed and thought about what the psychologist had told him: that he didn't have good radar for when others didn't share his interests and had to pay more attention to other people's "signals", their body language and silences. A muscle in his eye started to quiver.

"Lovely, son, but try not to let yourself get carried away so much, with your fish and whatnot, OK?"

That abrupt stabbing behind his eyes again. He gulped. He didn't want to say another word, just get upstairs as fast as he could. He remembered one of the psychologist's exercises, part of the social-skills training. He hadn't got that far yet, but had already read a few of the modules in his workbook. "You don't need to react to everything," it said. "Focus on you," he told himself.

When his mother asked what that was on the fish's stomach, he couldn't ignore it. He explained that it had probably been pecked or bitten, probably by a cormorant or some other bird, and that it needed rest and would make a full recovery. Then he started talking about tea. Later, at six, he'd make a nice omelette with bacon and cheese, warm up some soup and toast some bread. That seemed to satisfy her. She laughed and teased him, calling him her game warden, her fish whisperer, her doctor-fish doctor.

He smiled absently as unwanted images of the girl drifted through his mind again. Warm blood thrummed in his ears; he made a futile attempt to ignore his drumming heart. He needed to be alone, upstairs, he thought, then he could do his exercises. That way he would learn how to deal with it, how to manage his behaviour, the habits he could break. I am not bad, he thought, it's the actions I'm learning to control. So he blurted that he was going up to his room and she replied that she'd watch a bit of telly. But halfway up the stairs he already regretted being so short with her. I'll be nicer tonight, he thought, more sociable. I'll cook so well, take my time, make it up to her.

Through the floor he heard his mother's footsteps as she walked from the TV to the sofa and back again. She said something he couldn't make out to the dog. Jonathan gritted his teeth, got a layer of fresh water into the tank and connected the pump. Immediately a quiet bubbling sound filled the room into the furthest corners. The sounds from downstairs were diluted, spreading and subsiding until they were just a quiet hum, a distant murmur. Even though they didn't disappear completely, he still sighed with relief and felt almost like the new sound, the soft bubbling, was streaming out of his own body.

He quickly shrugged off those thoughts and set to work, excited to be able to refill the aquarium again. Routinely, as so often before, he fetched the scales from the bathroom and lifted up the fish, staring excitedly at the trembling needle and establishing that it weighed 1,250 grams. Not enough for an adult male tench of this length. "But I'll build you up again," he whispered; with good care he'd make it healthy again.

In the back of his workbook he drew up a schedule: every morning at six, just before work, and in the afternoon at 2.45, just after work, he would check the water temperature and cool it; 18 degrees was his target—everything over 23 had to be avoided. He would feed it mornings and evenings, and put that in his schedule: 6 a.m. and 9.30 p.m.: water fleas, sweetcorn, wrigglers, snails, dog food. With a bit of cheese now and then, he hoped to get its weight up.

He filled the aquarium some more and lowered the fish into it. In the water it looked heavier than it really was. It sank a good bit then slowly floated back up, its head almost against the glass. Jonathan squatted down in front of the tank and caught its gaze. It looked sad, he thought, but proud too. With his lips pressed together, he peered at the fish for a while and eventually felt an urge to talk to it, to explain himself. As if the fish too had found him guilty. Again he thought about his guilt feelings. The psychologist had told him that experiencing guilt feelings was part of having a normally developed conscience. Things didn't go the way I wanted them to, he thought, and that hurts. But this is my second chance—that was what the lawyer said, and he repeated the words in his head. If I do everything better than I have ever done before, he added, maybe I'll make it all up. This thought flashed through his mind with a brief feeling of satisfaction.

He turned back to the fish, whose head looked larger and larger through the gleaming glass. Sadder too. Jonathan's satisfaction gradually trickled out of him, making way for tension, as if a membrane inside his head had been drawn taut and could rupture at any moment. "I know the tank is small," he said. "And that you're imprisoned. But you're safe here." He listened to his own words and hoped it was enough.

For a while the fish floated dead still in the tank. Then it let itself drift along for a short distance in the gentle stream of bubbles from the air pump. It had turned away from Jonathan, but now turned back. A little later it swam slowly along the glass front of the aquarium, its whole body shining in the glow of the lights. Jonathan swallowed. Maybe this was how it had to be. The two of us together, he thought, and stayed sitting there dead still as if to let the moment solidify in time. Suddenly he smelt the sweat slowly trickling down his face and realized he'd forgotten to turn on the fan. He walked over to it and switched it on. So much for lying down on the floor and letting it blow air over his whole body. Now there wasn't enough time. He still had to give all the aquarium accessories a good scrub, then hoover downstairs.

First, he tore a blank sheet out of his exercise book with therapy notes, smoothed it out on the floor, used his ruler to draw long lines at right angles, then divided the horizontal axis into twenty-one blocks. Three times seven days, that should be enough time for him to nurse the fish back to health. He noted the tench's current weight a little bit up from the bottom of the vertical axis. The line would rise up from this point. But how much? Not knowing just how much the final weight should be, he left this axis blank for the time being.

Sitting cross-legged on the floor with the graph by his side, he studied it and the fish in turn and caught himself imagining the girl sitting opposite him, her mouth slightly open, her eyes fixed on the sheet of paper, then looking up at him or the fish. He would have liked to have shown her the neatly drawn graph, explaining that he was on the right path, looking after the fish but doing his exercises at the same time. Could she remove his guilt? He thought of the empathy exercise he'd done with the psychologist. What was important was picking up on other people's emotions, feeling what they were feeling. Those were the words the psychologist had used. It was important.

He got the workbook out as well and read what he himself had written about it. Feeling for others, sympathizing, helping. He repeated it to himself. This evening he'd look for a plaster for the girl to show how caring he was.

While sitting there looking thoughtfully at the fish in the tank, he suddenly noticed that the direction of its eyes seemed to diverge slightly. He crawled up to the glass and studied the almost luminescent orange-red eyes. It was like the fish could see more than normal. He was awed by the strength in its sturdy tail, even in this weakened state. Little drops flew up when it slapped the water and suddenly it seemed not just to see more, but to be able to do more than normal animals too.

"You know a lot, don't you?" he whispered to the fish, and felt his pulse throbbing in his temples. It wasn't something he could explain, but he had a strange feeling that there was a reason for all of this. His mother would have seen it as a sign from God, but not him. He thought it was something else, something too big or too complicated to understand. "You've come to help me," he continued. The blood rose from his throat to his cheeks. He froze for a moment, waiting to see if the fish would react, but it kept looking past him with its splayed eyes. "Are you going to help me?" he asked. It made him feel a bit stupid, but the question still meant something to him. It still had an impact.

He got out his animal book and read that the tench's scientific name was *Tinca tinca*. The reason it had been called the doctor or the physician fish was that people thought its skin and slime were medicinal and attributed healing powers to the fish. He read about a peasant woman who had used a tench to heal a wound on her hand and a tench that had cured and revitalized the carp in a pond just by its presence. "Will you help me?" he asked again. "Will you promise?" It felt right. But a little later he felt agitated again and returned to the plan he'd worked out with the psychologist. The warning-sign chart with its three phases. He looked at phase one, the phase in which things were going well. He was in that phase now—where else? Under "thoughts" he read what he had written one of those nights in his cell: "Not worrying about unnecessary things." Feelings: "Relaxed, calm." Behaviour: "Doing my own thing within the limits of decency and law." And after that: "What can I do?" Here he read: "Mind my own business and keep to myself. Stick to agreements." He wanted to expand on this and wrote: "Take care of my fish. Drink coffee and play cards with my mother." And also: "I keep my surroundings tidy."

At two minutes past six he started cooking: soup and an omelette. At six thirty-three he sat down to eat with his mother. Just after eight he was strolling through the deserted, mostly demolished neighbourhood with the dog. He felt calm and unhurried. It was still hot—a dry, stony heat hanging over the expanse of sand. Sunday evening. This evening, he suddenly remembered, at twenty past eight, in five minutes, his mother's favourite quiz show was on. The quiz show they had watched together for years. That came under leisure activities and seemed like a good, safe pastime. And also a way of distracting himself. Chasing off unwanted thoughts, that was how he pictured it, so they'd take flight like a flock of harried birds, scattered by the excited voices from the television. Fortunately, he had to work tomorrow too, he thought. His activities in the factory were the very best way of making sure he steered his ideas and all the things that could arise inside his head in the right direction.

Coming through the door, he could already hear the theme tune of the show he and his mother hadn't been able to watch together for so long. His mother was sitting on the sofa with a bowl of crisps.

"Just in time," she said, smiling at him. She had her feet up on a stool in front of her, her hands clasped under her bosom. He sat down next to her, intent on making a pleasant evening of it.

The first round started. Something about sport, a question about a government minister. At the third question, he asked, "Shall we join in?" And she said, "Lovely, it's been so long since we did that."

He'd made some more squash with ice and the cubes clicked quietly against each other when he filled their glasses. His mother already had a glass of sweet wine on the side table next to her.

He settled back on the sofa, his hands on the cushion he'd pulled up against himself, his fingers tightly interlaced. His mother slid over towards him. Have some fun now, he thought, it's eight twenty-four; nine o'clock it'll be over, just thirty-six minutes. Then the last bit of washing-up, air her bedroom and go upstairs.

"What are we going to win?" he asked. This was their game, almost as far back as he could remember. They fantasized about what they would win if they were standing there, guessing the contents of the prize boxes on the telly. And they told each other what they would like to have and where they'd put their new possessions.

"A microwave?" he asked, and his mother said, "Yes, that would be lovely in the new house, when we move."

"Yes."

A couple on TV had just won a trip to Paris.

"A fridge," he said, thinking of their current fridge, which often left a puddle on the floor in front of it.

"What's it look like?"

"Big and white, with an enormous crisper that keeps all the vegetables fresh for a really long time."

"Lovely," his mother laughed. She drank some wine, slurping now and then so he heard the sound of the liquid and air passing through her teeth. He remembered that before he'd only been able to sit there and think, "That sound has to stop," but not now: now he could handle anything. For a moment he concentrated on his shoulder muscles, making sure they stayed relaxed, and straightened his back.

His mother leant towards him, ever closer. Her eyes were greyish blue with tiny veins in the whites, branching in all directions. He could see flecks of a darker blue in her iris and shallow wrinkles in her skin. While his mother stared at the screen, he thought about the patterns they formed. This makes her happy, he told himself. Playing cards with him, watching the telly, she doesn't like to be alone. And he stayed calm. Try not to think about the fish, he told himself. Put your head down, let things happen. Just sitting here and saying what she likes to hear is good as long as you stay calm. I will ignore the loud, sometimes unexpected noises and the sunlight that is still shining in through the windows. Nothing upsets me; I'm just sitting here.

"And what else?" She meant the fridge, he realized after a second.

"Lots of compartments."

He thought about the kind of buzz the fridge they were going to win would make. A low, quiet buzz. That was good to think about.

"Wait a minute," he said after a while, standing up. A sigh escaped his lips. He wanted to do it differently after all, properly. In the hall, next to the phone, and after that in the kitchen, he searched for a pad, but couldn't find one anywhere. Then he went up to his room, grabbed his exercise book from under his pillow, carefully tore out a page, pulled open the table drawer, took out the pen and the ruler, and closed the drawer again. Downstairs, he knelt down at the table and started drawing up lines, two columns, one for her answers and one for his.

"Son, don't take it so seriously." She started to laugh. "There's no need to be so serious about it."

He laid the sheet of paper to one side, sat down, closed his eyes for a moment and opened them again. I'll keep breathing calmly and keep thinking, he thought. I mustn't take it personally, let things take their own course, don't contradict her. I'm fine sitting here on this sofa. Time is passing slowly, but it's passing.

"It's just a bit of fun, Jonny," she said a few more times. "It's just a game."

He resisted the temptation to stand up. His hands were folded together on his stomach. Now and then he put the tip of his tongue between his front teeth and bit down on it softly, or slowly let the spit build up in his mouth before silently swallowing.

Now he heard whooping and cheering from the TV. Someone shouted the word "roast" with a long, unnatural *r*, and suddenly the noise annoyed him. It was really loud. Like so many times before, he thought about how much noise there was in the world. Forcing itself on him. Suddenly he wanted to turn down the volume. But in his mind he could already hear her voice: "Hey, come on, son, I can hardly hear it like that."

She laughed softly at one of the host's jokes; the commercials began. He put on some coffee and refilled the crisp bowl. After a few minutes the show resumed. Even shriller, it seemed, even louder. He concentrated on his breathing. Inhale slowly, slowly exhale. Ten times. With his feet on the ground.

"A convection oven," his mother shouted. "Oven," he wrote under her name, and saw out of the corner of his eye that she was bending over towards him and reading what he was writing. He felt her breath on his face. Suddenly he stood up. "I have to eat something," he said, picking up an empty bowl and walking back to kitchen, where it occurred to him that the game they were playing was actually a bit weird. He'd played it for years, but suddenly it seemed different. In the past they'd spent hours sitting there coming up with things they wanted, things that never came and never would come, and he'd always stayed calm, even when he would have preferred being upstairs alone. This too was part of his life, he'd reasoned. But that no longer seemed appropriate. Maybe because his thoughts were wandering, because he couldn't stop thinking about the girl after seeing her from so close by. Or because of the time he'd spent in prison, and all the words the psychologist had used, the words that applied to him and made him feel so different from before. Or was it the workbook? The exercises demanded so much concentration they drained him almost completely.

He dished up some leftover omelette and bread for himself and went back to the living room, called Milk over and sat down on his own chair with the dog at his feet. He sniffed and tensed his back muscles again. He thought for a moment. Maybe it wasn't necessarily bad that something had changed about the game. He was just tired. That was why he couldn't keep his mind on it.

"Your turn," his mother said, and he nodded absently.

"Just a moment." Then, to get it over and done with, "Waterbed." He took a couple of bites, chewed carefully, then washed it down with a mouthful of squash. He manoeuvred a cube of ice between his teeth with his tongue and held it there, waiting with his mouth half open for it to melt a little, the cold passing down his spine, then cracking it in half with one hard bite. It's just a game, he thought. Enjoy it. Still, he couldn't stop brooding about how restless he felt and how detached from his mother and the things around him. It was all so different from how he'd imagined it. At half-nine he went upstairs, closed the door and got back to his workbook.

T HE NEXT MORNING, Monday, Jonathan started work.
Happily, because he hoped that regular workdays would
make it easier for him to get back into his old rhythm.

And for a while his old life did start rolling again as if nothing had ever happened. He got up at five and worked through
the day's programme calmly. Walking Milk, working until
half-two, taking the dog out a second time, helping his mother,
cooking, walking the dog again, doing his assignments, taking
care of the fish.

He spent the evenings sitting with his mother and each evening was the same as the one before. After tea she sat on the sofa
and watched TV. He sat on his chair and thought about things.
Time passed, then he went to make some coffee. He asked if
she wanted some too and she said, "Yes, lovely, son, nice." He
watched her, the way she drank and the light from the television gliding over her face, and saw thoughts passing through
his head as well. Often they would end up playing cards at the
kitchen table, the window open wide. They played elbow to
elbow. He endured it. Evening after evening.

Sometimes he saw her look at him and quickly avert her eyes.
Often she held the cross on her necklace between her thumb
and index finger to rub it cautiously. He wondered what was
going through her mind at times like that. As long as she saw
how hard he was working, how he was doing his very best. He
got the boxes and change of address cards. That pleased her.
How could it not?

But he also thought about that day with Betsy. Sometimes he got a sudden urge to walk over to his mother, lay a hand on her forehead and slide it down over her eyelids, as if that would be a way of reaching the place in her brain where the images and thoughts of that day were stored. As if he could wipe the stain away, like condensation on a window. She must know that something had happened with that child. He wanted her to just see the present, the person he was becoming. Someone better.

No matter what he was doing he was alert, watching her. He saw the toll the heat was taking on her body. She was coughing more; her breathing was getting more laboured. And every day he resolved to try even harder. To clean the house better, getting rid of the most ingrained dust, blowing the sand out of every chink and crack, sweeping, mopping.

He was relieved that they'd let him come back to work. It was because his dad had been the factory's head foreman for fifteen years and his grandfather had founded the company before that. Otherwise he was sure he might as well have written his job off.

They put him back in his regular spot on the line, the place in the back corner where he'd always worked, under the bluish fluorescent light. Nobody deigned to meet his gaze, but he felt the other men's eyes on him when he wasn't looking. Burning holes in his back. He shut them out by raising his shoulders, his head tucked down into the collar of his greasy, stinking oilskins.

Just when the sun was showing itself outside, the machine started up and the gutting began. A movement that was second nature to him, that seemed to flow automatically through his shoulders, hands and fingers. He pulled his Stanley knife out of the beam, put his gloves on and pushed earplugs into his ears to block the endless drone of the machinery, then spread his legs with his boots planted firmly on the floor to avoid slipping in the pool of rinsing water and slimy waste that would soon be washing around his feet. Tails, scales, guts.

During the breaks he kept aloof from everyone, like always. According to the psychologist, secluding himself was a "survival mechanism". That was what he called it. Everyone had survival mechanisms: there was nothing bad about it, it was normal. Good, even. And things got crowded inside his head faster than they did with other people. It was simply a question of taking what the psych called his "vulnerabilities" into account.

During the breaks he sat at the back of the canteen with a cup of coffee, reading *Nature* and staying out of any conversations. He wouldn't have known what to say anyway. The other workers were foreign to him: they had loud voices and smelt of booze and rolling tobacco; they talked about women and bars and complained about the boss. They couldn't wait until they could go home again. But he loved his job, the stream of actions that just kept coming: grabbing the fish from the belt, inserting the point of the knife in behind the gills and pulling it back towards him in one fluid movement, turning the fish over, repeating the same motion on the other side, and done, next. Often it felt like time was accelerating and at the same time draining away into the cuts he made in the skin with his knife. In moments like that the other men didn't seem to exist. And it would be like that every day. Over and over.

At half past two precisely his shift finished. In the small room behind the canteen he wrung his stiff, clammy body out of the oilskins, sprayed them and his boots with the high-pressure hose and strolled home through the heat in his overalls and boots. There he had a quick shower, took the dog for a walk, helped his mother and was in the kitchen cooking again at six. Frying the fish he'd been allowed to bring home that day. Cod, sole, gurnard or whiting. The grease specks on the stove, the spitting oil, the flour he rubbed over the fish, powdery soft on his hands.

And every day he worked in the workbook, twice a day, no matter how exhausted he was. He was determined to become better and he would. A better person. A new person.

For a few days he'd only seen the girl out of the corner of his eye. Sometimes, when he came home, she'd be sitting on her space hopper in the middle of the bare expanse. Other times he'd see her walking, dragging the hopper behind her like a reluctant animal. A few times he saw her on roller skates at the edge of the village, drawing long lines through her boredom in the narrow streets. Each time he made sure not to catch her eye, shooting quickly down a side street. He was concentrating on himself and his therapy.

Today, Thursday, he had worked on what the psychologist called the ABC. It was a way of understanding and controlling the choices you made and what happened in your life. You could expand it with a D, an E and an F, but the main thing was the ABC: the Activating Event, your Beliefs about it, and the Consequences. Beliefs could be rational or irrational beliefs and they led to healthy or unhealthy consequences. He'd drawn three parallel lines with his ruler and made a column for each row, a reassuring activity. It was all linked together like a chain, that was what he had learnt. Your feelings came from your beliefs and led to behaviour that had consequences. And then you had the events, things that happened to you. They were things you had no control over. But you could choose how to deal with them.

Now he had to give his own example of a behaviour chain. He thought about it, finding it difficult, gently gnawing the end of his pencil for a while. In the end he wrote down: "Activating event: mother can't breathe. Belief: I am responsible. Consequences: tense, worried, mistakes at work." What it came down to was learning how to change the beliefs that made you feel and act in certain ways. Breaking the chain.

He fleshed out his example, worked at it until he'd provided as much detail as he could, then finished off with a long relaxation exercise. Lying stretched out on his back on the floor with the cotton-wool plugs in his ears. His mother was watching TV; there was no one to disturb him. He concentrated his full attention on the inside of his skull. That was a place of calm. A state he'd been practising achieving.

It was like he could hear the quiet murmur of his blood; everything inside him was suddenly so quiet, and that gave him the courage to descend further into his body, the way he'd learnt in the visualization exercises. With his eyes closed he worked his way down, through his throat to his shoulders and into his chest. He held each spot for three seconds, breathed out and continued his journey. He saw his stomach, liver, all of his organs, and imagined them the way he knew them from the fish at the factory. The liver a gleaming purple, enclosed by a soft membrane, his intestines a greyish red, grainy. He pictured his cock, which seemed soft, friendly. Hesitantly he lowered his hand to it and felt it. His balls were soft too. All the energy seemed to have flowed out of them.

The past few days he'd made so much more progress than with the assignments they'd made him do in prison. It was like he'd raised himself up to a higher level, he thought proudly. Without any help from anyone else. The psychologist had insisted that it often took years before the treatment really began to have an effect. Before men learnt to divert their thoughts, as he put it. And then they still had to put it into practice. Sometimes it was beyond them and medication was the only solution. Anti-libido drugs. But not for him, he thought, while carefully wrapping his hand around his cock and rubbing it with his fingertips. It began to stiffen and swell, but even now his mind stayed clear.

The exercises worked on him so well. If this keeps up, he thought, maybe I'll be finished in a few weeks. He couldn't remember ever having felt this strong. Maybe he needed to test himself again. Just go and sit down somewhere near that girl. He saw her often enough at the playground.

He raised himself up slightly on his elbows. He just had to see what happened when he saw her again, he thought, and slumped back down on the floor. His breath left his mouth in a long sigh. That psychological report had felt like a constant weight pressing down on his chest. It said that the chance of a relapse, a repeat offence, was high in the short to medium term. But right now that seemed completely wrong. And to prove it he was going to do another exercise.

He sat down again at the small table, turned to an empty page and carried on from there. His hand was aching from all the writing; a muscle was quivering. He didn't let it distract him. "Breaking Free," it said in his workbook. "Think of an activity in your daily life where you later realized that you were asking too much of yourself." He thought about it until he heard his mother calling from downstairs. "Jon! Yoo-hoo!" And when he didn't respond immediately, "Jon, you going to make some coffee?"

"Five minutes, Mum." He wanted to carry on. It was about situations in which you demanded too much of yourself. Maybe that week last year when he did a lot of overtime. He put the earplugs back in and thought about it. Then began writing. He looked to the fish for help, and kept writing.

When he was finished, he made two cups of coffee and went to sit with his mother in the living room. "Thanks, son," she said. "Lovely."

T HE NEXT DAY at three o'clock on the dot Jonathan was alone and ambling over the sand and gravel where the blocks of flats had stood. It had been a hard day at work and he was exhausted, his shoulders aching. Sweating in the baking-hot air that was shimmering just above the ground.

When Betsy was still around, he often took Milk for walks in the dunes with her. But only to the first part; her parents wouldn't let her go any further. There was a big open field there where you could see rabbits hopping around even before twilight. He thought of the little squeaks she always made when she spotted one, just before covering her mouth with her hands in her astonishment, every time again, so he could only tell how big her smile was from the dimples in her cheeks and the wrinkles around her nose. He could be so envious of how free she was. Every evening he knew what was coming: she always acted the same, but he never got tired of seeing it.

But he would never do anything like that again, he thought, taking a child out of the village. That had been so stupid of him, so unbelievably stupid. He was only allowed to talk to the girl from next door up to the bench of the old playground with the swing, where he had seen her sitting yesterday. That was the absolute limit. And no longer than five or so minutes.

Suddenly he thought of one of his very first sessions with the psychologist. In his first weeks in jail he'd constantly brooded over how it could have happened. How could he have let the horrific fantasies that had slowly crept into his head become reality? He pictured himself sitting at the table across from the psychologist, his fat file between them, and felt the fear and the shame.

"Offence analysis"—that was what they were doing, going back to the exact moment, just before it happened. He would have to do it again later, the psychologist explained, in the psychiatric hospital. He was better off being prepared. He'd even have to give a presentation about his offence to all the patients and staff. Taking responsibility for what he'd done, that was what they called it, taking responsibility. Everyone had to. Just thinking about the hospital paralysed him with fear. He thought about the bustle and racket, the unexpected fights.

But now he was trying to do it, making his first attempt to sketch out a presentation, sitting at a table with the psychologist one afternoon. He struggled to answer the man's questions, but often there was just silence in his head, he couldn't explain himself.

He had actually wanted to be the one asking the questions. He wanted to know how he could have turned out so different from the person he'd always thought he was. Often his mother's words sprang to mind, her claim that everyone was born perfect, created by God. If that was true, how come he, whenever he thought about what had happened, no longer felt like he was one whole? It was like his head had been crammed too full, year in, year out. Too many words, voices, questions, situations. It didn't fit. Sometimes it got so full it seemed like his head was starting to quietly tear, to break, like he was falling apart.

He often sat silently at the table, staring awkwardly at his hands for long periods, ashamed that he had so little to say. Never before had he felt so lost. The days and nights flowed together and he just sat there in his cell. Alone. Waiting.

"I understand that it's difficult to talk about," the psychologist had said. "Let's try to write it down instead, together, to see what exactly happened." He'd given him the workbook, the exercise book, printouts with exercises. "Increasing tension before the offence" was written next to the exercise that first time. He had to learn to know himself better, "to raise the alarm" sooner, "to learn to read his body". Together they would work out a list of warning signs. The section about tension was illustrated with a cartoon of a barrel that was getting fuller and fuller. In the last picture it started to bubble and overflow.

"Try to keep a record of your tensions every day for seven days," the psychologist suggested. "When does the tension increase, when does it decrease?"

He'd nodded and gathered up the papers, forcing a smile, uncomfortable. He would do his best, definitely. He always did.

The psychologist nodded too, looking at him over the top of his glasses and making notes, which he then stored away in the folder. Silence.

After a while all those pages about him were bound together with a thick rubber band. He had stared at it disbelievingly. "Is it really possible?" he'd wanted to ask. "Will I become whole again?" And: "How am I going to get by in the hospital? What will I have to do to survive?" But he didn't say a word, he just slowly rubbed the knuckle of his left thumb with his right and waited. The man took off his glasses and folded them up. "Next week we'll continue."

That evening he'd drawn up a graph in his cell. A tension graph. He took a ruler, pens and pencils, paper, and drew up a grid. On the left, a scale from one to ten; along the bottom, the days. And every day he studied his workbook. He noticed that the words and the tables were keeping him company, even though he didn't always know just what he was doing.

And when the next week came, he at least had a neatly completed graph with him. He'd even joined up the tension levels to make a smooth, descending curve. And the psychologist seemed satisfied. He smiled. "Fantastic, Jonathan. It's going well, isn't it?"

Yes, he was making progress, he thought, glowing with pride. Maybe it was just a question of submitting. Trusting in science, and putting his fate in the hands of psychology. Then everything would get better.

There was no one around the square in the middle of the demolished neighbourhood. He sat down on a bench. He had taken the coarse-toothed comb with him and was combing Milk when the girl appeared out of nowhere and came up next to him. Although he'd been expecting her, he felt that blow on his neck again, his muscles stiffening and contracting. He saw her lips moving before her words got through to him.

"Hey, can I do that?"

He braced himself. It had been four days since he'd seen the strange girl with the sandy ponytail up close. All the times he'd wanted to go looking for her outside, he'd managed to divert his thoughts. He'd got a grip on himself, bent over his workbook and instructed himself about how later, when he saw her, he would keep everything under control. And now he was already holding out a hand to pass her the comb. That wasn't the agreement, Jonathan, he told himself, pulling his hand back. I don't have to do everything she asks. Set your own limits, the psychologist had explained, that's important. Then things won't boil over so quickly. That was literally what he'd said, boil over, as if his head was a saucepan of milk. I set my own limits, he repeated, silently mouthing the words. "No." He bent forward and drew the comb through the dog's coat. Looking sideways at her.

"Fine." She blew away the stray lock of hair, which immediately fell back down over her forehead. She shrugged, sat next to him on the bench, made a move as if she was going to slide over towards him, then changed her mind and slid down onto the ground.

Now he was looking down at her. There was a small mole like a pencil dot on her right ear lobe. She was wearing the top he'd seen her in a few days ago, the one with the flower, but had got a dirty mark on the shoulder in the meantime. Her towelling shorts were tight around her bottom: they must pinch in the crotch, he thought, but was already averting his eyes. She had a book with her and began to read. He could see out of the corner of his eye that she was muttering silently and she kept raising her index finger to her mouth to moisten the tip and turn the page.

Her not saying anything delivered him up to his own thoughts. And in that moment he felt that tension again, the seed of fury. What was he doing? Why shouldn't he let the girl comb Milk for a while? Wasn't that actually part of a normal interaction with children? In the meantime, the dog had lain down, stretched out towards the girl and rested his sluggish head on her thigh, eyes half closed and luxuriating in the attention. She was saying something to him, but softly, and Jonathan couldn't make out what it was. Her whispering disappeared in Milk's coat.

"Here, you do the rest," he said, giving her the comb.

"OK." She hardly looked at him, getting up on her knees and edging round a little so she could bend over the dog and slowly pull the teeth of the comb through his hair. He could hear her breathing.

He managed to read the title of her book: *What Do You Know about Animals?*

She followed his gaze and looked up proudly. "Dad gave it to me." She sniffed, studying him for a moment through her hair. "I looked up that fish of yours. Tench," she giggled. "But I don't think it's in it."

"You don't see them here often."

"Do they need to be protected?"

"Maybe. I don't know."

"Cause I'm starting a club to protect animals."

"A club?" He gave her an awkward smile.

"Yeah, a club. But I have to hurry up," she said, "because we're leaving soon. Thank God." She looked around and sniffed. "There's nothing to do here, no kids at all. It is *sooooo* boring. A real shithole."

He looked down at her, so close by. He noticed that he found it difficult when she talked like that, like recently about her mother in the bar. That coarseness didn't suit her. She turned back towards him and puckered her forehead into a frown while looking at him. It was like her face grew softer and more beautiful every time he saw her. In the weak, grey light she looked even younger, even more innocent. He chewed on the inside of his cheek.

Don't look at me like that, he thought. Just don't. And to himself: Don't think so much. Don't get hung up on your thoughts. "Thoughts come and go like waves in a river," it said in the workbook, everything passes.

"I'm not allowed to say where we're going," she said. "Or when. Nobody's allowed to know where we live, except me and Mum, of course. And Milk and your mother. You're not allowed to tell anyone either!"

I never talk to anyone was on the tip of his tongue. Nobody knows me. But he rubbed the knuckle of his left thumb with his right and hoped it would calm him. She was looking straight at him. He saw an expression he couldn't place. Often it was better not to say anything. Words never solved anything.

"Dad's definitely not allowed to know."

"What?"

"Where we live. That's what Mum says. Now you're going to ask where Dad is, of course. But I'm not going to say that either." She shook her head and the lock of hair fell to one side of her face.

She'd said her piece. Now and then she whispered something to the dog, and when she did, he felt that she was looking at him. He thought about all the things she'd just said and felt an overwhelming desire to leave it at that—he already knew too much. He had enough on his plate with himself.

Suddenly he wanted to be gone; he was already half standing, but then he sat down again. He knew that if he left now, he'd regret it and want to come back again. Still, he made another attempt, rising again and gently gripping Milk by the scruff of his neck. "Come on, boy, it's getting late."

She started to protest. "Hey, I haven't finished combing him yet!"

"That's more than enough."

"You're mean. He'll get hot like this. It's sad."

Sad. He thought of the word that came up in the workbook so often: empathy. He wasn't insensitive, far from it; if anyone was caring towards others, it was him. But he still couldn't see why she thought it was sad. How were you supposed to know what others were thinking or feeling anyway? The dog looked happy enough to him. "It's not that bad."

The furrows in her forehead grew deeper. Her nose puckered. He could see her nostrils quivering. Did she really care that much about the dog? She'd wrapped her arms around his neck and pulled him onto her lap as best she could. Milk didn't put up any resistance. With her he was completely docile. He looked at the dog, sprawled out on the ground and breathing heavily. "All right then, just a bit more."

She turned away again and he stretched his back, looking at the houses that lined the cleared area. Empty windows, he thought. Blind eyes.

The vertebrae in her neck, the curves of her ears, everything, it was all coming much too close, but he stayed sitting. I have to practise, he thought. Maybe that was best. Look, he thought, without knowing who he was addressing, look at how I'm sitting here. He thought back on that river and letting it flow. Look at her and let time pass.

"But he's sorry now," he heard the girl say after a while. Her voice sounded different and he asked, "What?"

"He said so himself."

"Who?"

"Dad. For leaving. He calls me sometimes. He's sad."

She was now bent completely over the dog, her cheek pressed against his coat. It made her look terribly sweet. He tried to concentrate on something else and forced himself to look at all the things that weren't right about her, all the things that weren't beautiful. The sun lit up the grimy fabric of her top; he could count her vertebrae through it. He thought of the slight smell of sweat he'd just caught.

The dog gave a deep growl of satisfaction and rolled onto his side. With long, careful strokes she pulled the comb through Milk's hair, pressing down on his back with her free hand. Jonathan stared at her rough, chewed nails. Tufts of hair came loose and drifted over the tiles as if they were lost and looking for a hiding place.

"Mum says they're a pain in the arse," she said. "All of them. The lady from child welfare's the worst. I think so too."

He heard her voice on the edge of his thoughts, but closed himself off from it. Maybe there wasn't that much to be afraid of after all. What could happen out here anyway? And the girl was smart and strong, he could see that. Her eyes were clear and when she turned towards him she met his gaze straight on. But her smile was insipid, not joyful. That had to change. He wanted her to feel safe. It was worrying. In the meantime, she changed the subject.

"Can I come and look at the fish sometime?"

"Maybe."

"Tomorrow?"

"Some other time."

"Is it still sick? Are you looking after it properly?"

All these questions! He told her that of course he was looking after it properly, thinking at the same time that it was pathetic that he apparently felt the need to defend himself. "Yes, it already weighs 1.4 kilograms. At first it only weighed one and a quarter," he said firmly.

"It had been bitten, right?"

"It's getting stronger every day."

She looked relieved. A very slight breeze had come up. It passed over the skin of his arms and made his hairs stand on end. He smoothed them down again.

"I really hate it," she said, "when animals suffer. I'm glad you're not cruel to animals. I don't like people who are cruel to animals." Her hands moved slowly over her throat and started picking at the material of her top.

"I knew someone and he hit a dog I knew too. I'd never hit my dog. I think it's so mean when people do that. Or if they hit children or are mean to them. And then later they don't say sorry. If you say sorry, it's different."

She was quiet for a moment, looking down at the paving stones and then straight ahead, squinting into the sunlight. "I think it's sad too if a horse has to live in a stable and do whatever people want it to. And when animals die and they get, what's it

called, not buried but thrown away or put in the rubbish bin.
I think that's sad."

I have to go, he thought.

"Before, when Dad was still living with us and we didn't
move all the time, I had lots of pets. Guess how many."

He looked up and around. Delicate threads of cloud were
floating slowly past, just over the rooftops, the sun already
descending in the west. A purple glow lit the sky. It was a very
mysterious light.

"In my club we're going to protect animals. I'm going to
write the club rules. I'm really good at rules." She picked up her
book and started leafing through it. OK, Jonathan told himself,
you listen to the rules and then you leave.

"In the house we were in before this one, I made rules for
my room. I hung them up on the door and copied them out on
a piece of paper I take with me wherever I go. Listen."

She took a crumpled sheet of paper out from between the
pages of the book and started to read, solemnly reciting the
rules one after the other.

"My Room Rules:
—nobody is allowed to barge into my room without
asking first
—I decide for myself what my room looks like
—if I am asleep, don't wake me up
—if you're angry, you are not allowed to shout inside
my room or break things
—in my room you are not allowed to hit anyone or
squeeze them or be mean
—don't just barge into my room if I'm doing something
—if you take something from my room you always
have to put it back and not lose it."

You don't want to know all of this, Jonathan, he thought. The girl was sitting motionless in front of him and staring down at her own words. She's alone, he thought, but it's not my fault. He cleared his throat and stood up. "Milk and I have to go now," he said, breaking the silence.

She turned at once and looked up at him. "No, don't go. I've got other stuff I can read too. I've got stories. When I grow up I'm going to be a writer and I practise in this exercise book." She had pulled a thin exercise book with a blue cover out from between the pages of her book and now opened it. "I write down everything that happens to me, look."

He saw that she had drawn up columns, just like he always did.

"Tench," she had written with three points beneath it: "Family of the carp. Also called the doctor fish. As big as a pike."

He nodded. "I have to go help my mother," he said.

"My mother works so much she's hardly ever here." She looked miserable. "She's at that stupid bar all day. She doesn't even have time to cook any more."

"What do you eat then?"

Why are you asking that? he thought immediately. What are you still doing here?

"Bread. It's not like I don't like it or anything. With peanut butter, that's my favourite."

Part of him wanted to ask her lots more questions, but it was getting late and he felt like he had to go and not stay here talking to her any longer. The five minutes were up ages ago.

"Look," she said suddenly, holding her ring finger out to him. She was wearing a small, cheap ring. "Dad gave it to me. He won it on the shooting gallery at the fair."

The light on the copper-coloured fleck in her right eye was now so incredibly beautiful he had to catch his breath. I am flesh, he thought. I am flesh. But I can control the flesh. He thought about what he had read yesterday evening on the scrap of paper on which his mother had copied out some quotes from the Bible. She'd left it lying open with her bookmark in place and the piece of paper covered in writing. It was about how you can live according to the flesh or the spirit, and that if you set your mind on the spirit you'll have life and peace.

He'd put it in his pocket and read it over and over again, learning sentences off by heart. It went on to say that you weren't condemned to sins in the flesh, but you had to say no. No to desire.

"I really have to go home now. Say goodbye to Milk."

He was in bed lying on his back. It was dark. The curtains were open. In the distance the moon was no more than a thumbnail, a splinter of bone. He was tired. Nagging backache. For a very long time he lay still with his hands on his stomach. Breathing. He felt like he could be proud of himself. He hadn't stayed out on the square with her for too long and he hadn't had any weird thoughts about her. But it was still disturbing that he was already thinking about her again now. About what she'd told him and about her mother hardly ever being there. He never saw her around the house either. That wasn't right. The child didn't have anywhere to relax, he thought, and everyone needs to be able to relax, to have somewhere safe. Animals and people too.

His thoughts began to drift. How could it be that he had his thoughts under such good control one minute and they'd set off in a direction of their own the next? Did he worry about other people too much? The psychological report said he wasn't good at seeing things from other people's perspectives, but that seemed completely wrong. He was actually constantly worried. About his mother, about the girl. Just then he'd looked at her wound and seen that it was closed, but given her a plaster anyway in case the scab came off. And he took so much work off his mother's hands: he cooked and tomorrow he'd start packing the boxes, and by playing cards with her every evening he made her happy, despite being completely indifferent to it himself. He did all of that for others. The only one who worried about him was his mother. And maybe Milk. Though he wasn't sure if animals were even capable of that, being concerned about others.

Right now the dog was snoring softly on the floor next to him. Jonathan dangled his hand out of the bed and stroked his head. His thoughts started off again. He could see the girl very clearly now. The outline of her shoulders visible under her top. The material clinging to her backbone. She was skinny. He wondered if his helping her a little bit more could do any harm. As long as he kept his distance, it would be OK, wouldn't it? Surely there couldn't be anything risky about giving her something to eat?

An hour later he still hadn't fallen asleep. It had been such a good day, and now this. From downstairs he could still hear the drone of the TV. He knew his mother slept badly too. If he went downstairs for a glass of milk in the night, he'd find her sitting in front of the telly in her dressing gown more often than not.

He turned from one side to the other for a while before finally falling asleep, but woke with a start a few hours later, wet with sweat. He immediately sat up straight. Was that a bang? No, it's nothing. He stood up, walked over to the window, stared into the dark for a moment, then went into the bathroom for a drink of water. The alarm clock said two thirty. Back in bed he felt his heartbeat slowly settle. After a few minutes he fell asleep again.

T O JONATHAN'S SURPRISE he found the door ajar when he came home on Monday afternoon. He'd taken the bus to the pet shop and bought water plants for the fish. Why was the door open? He was sure he'd locked it. Maybe his mother had let Milk out into the front yard and hadn't closed it properly afterwards? He looked around, but there was nobody in sight. Slowly he walked into the hall and found his mother asleep in front of the TV with the sound turned down.

He turned it off and left her to sleep on the sofa. That way he could be alone for a moment in the quiet without anyone asking him anything. He pulled off his boots and walked through the hall in his socks. Just when he was about to go upstairs, he saw something big and round in the dark corner under the stairs. The space hopper.

This is not good, he thought. Not good at all. His throat tightened, restricting his breathing. He wiped his sweaty hair away from his forehead with both hands, crossed his arms to hike up his overalls, stood still and looked around. She was upstairs, of course. The girl had seen that the door was open and gone up to look at the fish. He took a deep breath. And another. His pulse was pounding in his temples. He thought of the workbook. Some situations you simply just had to learn to bear, he knew that. But for the moment he'd forgotten which ones they were. And he couldn't go and look it up now, it was upstairs in his room. What else was there? The screwed-up tissues in the waste-paper basket, his workbook and the exercise book on the table. Pen, pencil, ruler. As long as she didn't touch anything.

He closed his eyes and stood there for a while. His hairline was itching. Self-confidence, he thought. The book said you needed self-confidence. You needed to feel strong. To banish fear. "Fear is a poor counsellor," he said quietly, and opened his eyes again. You mustn't let it take control. Come on! He chased the doubts out of his mind, concentrated on his breathing—long breaths, deep breaths—walked upstairs and stopped in front of the door.

There in the silence he heard, very softly, the murmur of a child's voice. He couldn't make out the words, but it was her, as he'd guessed, no doubt about it. Was she talking to the fish? Wheezing quietly, he pushed the door open and let his eyes adjust to the semi-darkness. There she was, on her knees in front of the aquarium.

"Hi, Jonathan," she smiled, then turned back to the fish. "Look what it's doing." She pressed her nose even harder against the glass. He watched it steam over.

He stayed there for a moment, motionless, holding his breath, numb and vacant. And then he had a strange thought. That it wouldn't actually matter what happened here. That everything that happened in his room would trickle away into nothing, just like the time that leaked away at work, never to return. He thought about it for a moment and wondered if he shouldn't see it differently, as something that had happened for a reason, a sign, an opportunity. Yes, he thought, it is different. It's a test. I have to stay alert. See how my body reacts. He scarcely dared to move, but still edged a little closer to stand there awkwardly, a few steps behind her with the water plants in one hand. There was a particular smell in the room, he noticed. A smell that was different from usual. She was still staring at the fish.

"How'd you get in here?" he asked.

For a moment she didn't respond. He heard the click and scratch of birds' feet in the gutter, quiet cooing. Pigeons. Then she looked at him. "The door was open. And now I'm looking at this beautiful fish. I was scared it might not be doing too well." She looked up at him and gave a cautious smile. "Its wound's got smaller. Did you see?"

He didn't move. After a while he noticed that the silence in his bedroom was different with her there. Like a held breath. Sunk in thought and staring in turn at the motionless girl and the light shining in through the low window, he imagined the prison psychologist. His long, bony face and piercing eyes. It seemed very far away right now, as if something in the room was blocking it. The light, her presence, or the carpet muffling the sounds. He found it almost impossible to picture the two of them working on the offence analysis together. He'd have to look up his notes later and read through them. But now he had to let it all go. Let it go, he said quietly to himself. Let it go.

"You didn't tell me what it's called," she said after a while. Her breath was still misting the glass of the aquarium, she was sticking that close to it.

"It doesn't have a name."

"That's weird."

He walked over to her. Now that he was confronted with what the workbook called a "high-risk situation" the best thing was to see what effect it had on him. Carefully, so as not to make too much sound, he took the folding chair, sat down a safe distance away and took a deep breath, feeling the air come in through his nostrils, find its way to his throat and the bottom of his lungs, then flow back up to his mouth. Ten inhalations, ten exhalations.

Minutes passed without either of them saying a word. He sneaked an anxious glance in her direction. She was sitting unmoving in front of the tank, her lips pursed, her mouth slightly open. Lying on the floor next to her he now saw the animal book he'd seen her with before. He waited for a moment to see if something was going to happen, but nothing changed. The girl just stared at the fish, which was floating big and silent on the other side of the slightly misted glass, which seemed to enlarge it even more. Jonathan sighed. Slowly he blew out some more breath.

"Is it a girl?" she asked and—studying her tentatively from behind, her dangling ponytail, her running shorts, her top, the line of her back, her neck—he began to explain that it was a male, pointing out its large lower fins and the thick outer ray on the ventral fins. The girl got up on her knees and craned her neck for a better view.

"Its Latin name is *Tinca tinca*," he said, and she repeated it to herself, "Tinca," and then again, "Tinca."

"It's a shy, gentle fish." His gaze glided over the tank. "It likes peace and quiet. If there's too much noise or if other animals get too close, it hides in the mud. It gets scared easily. Then we have to leave it alone."

"She's lying on the mud now too. Is she scared now too?"

He ignores the "she" and explains that tench don't cope well in the heat. That they sometimes hide in the mud because it's cooler there.

"That's sad. Is it too hot today too?"

"Yes."

He listens to himself talking. It's going well. It's like he's outside himself and watching this man who's explaining things, or standing behind himself and looking over his own shoulder. But he can still feel everything that's happening inside his body.

The way his heart is pumping blood, the arteries throbbing in his throat, the burning of his cheeks. He has to stay sitting here like this, he tells himself, sitting perfectly motionless, not doing anything. He hardly dared to move anyway, scared of ruining it. It was fantastic. She seemed genuinely interested and stayed so calm. He'd never experienced anything quite like her quiet concentration. He thought of the term "protective factors". Couldn't calm like this be a protective factor too? It was like a warm fluid streaming through his veins.

"It's a very special animal too," he went on. "Before, in the old days, they used to think that it…" He searched for the best words to explain the fish's powers to her. "That if you were sick, the fish could make you better. You only needed to touch its skin and then you'd recover, just like that."

"Really?" He saw the wonder in her eyes. "From what? What diseases?"

"It didn't matter, anything." He told her about the peasant woman who was healed by touching a tench, the school of carp that got better. She kept her eyes fixed on him while he talked.

When he'd finished, a silence fell. A very different kind of silence from the ones he was used to. Not uncomfortable, but soft, and it lightened the tension in his shoulders. He suddenly felt stronger than ever before and observed the girl, still on her knees before the tank, closely once again. She had closed her eyes in deep concentration. Her soft lips were still slightly open; her front teeth were showing again.

As if he had said something about them, she touched her chipped tooth with one finger. "I was supposed to go to the dentist with Dad for this tooth. But he left and Mum didn't have any money. We were maybe going to go during the holidays, but we haven't yet. Could Tinca make my tooth better too? If I'm around her a lot?"

"Maybe."

He walked around to the other side of the tank with the bag of water plants, and when he went to open it, she asked, "Can I do that?"

He hesitated. If she dropped it, it would make a mess. A dirty carpet, plants on the floor, water everywhere. It didn't bear thinking about. He looked at her and didn't know what to do. She was frowning and looked serious. He passed her the bag, which she took gently with both hands. "Be careful opening it."

She peeled the plastic down like a sock. Again he saw the tiny tip of her tongue sticking out between her lips. He moved away and took up position a few steps behind her. When she bent over the tank to let the plants slide into it, the material of her shorts crept up between the cheeks of her bottom. He looked away quickly.

After they had sat next to the aquarium for a while watching the fish swimming between its new plants, she started talking about her mother again. About how much money she was saving and how everything was going to be better in their new house, soon, in the city, close to her school, but she didn't know where that was yet. After that she told him about her father. "When he was still living with us, he used to work really hard. Sometimes he worked so hard he got sick."

"Oh." He didn't know how to react to that, but she was already talking again.

"And then I'd take care of him."

"You?"

"Yes, me. I'm old enough," she said. "I'm good at it." He noticed that her voice had changed again. She looked sad. The furrows in her forehead grew deeper.

"Would you like to give Tinca something to eat?" he asked to distract her. With his hands tensing up again, he pressed his fingertips against each other and bent his fingers until the cracking of the joints provided some relief. For a moment he was lost in a confusing web of thoughts. He thought through everything she had just told him with mixed feelings: concern and pride at once. Was she hoping he would help her? And how was he supposed to do that? He pondered for a moment. Didn't that mean she trusted him?

"Would you like to give him something to eat?" he asked again, whereupon she nodded and flashed a faint smile. She looked at her feet awkwardly, then sat down, pulled her hairband out of her hair, ran her fingers through her ponytail, then tied it up again. When he got up to get the canister of fish food, she started talking again. Her voice had taken on yet another tone. "I bet you're like all the others."

He stiffened and rubbed his throat, clammy and warm, combed his hair with his fingers and stood there without speaking. Just when he'd thought he'd understood what was going through her mind, she said something like this. He felt like walking away, fleeing the situation, but he kept his distance and looked over her head and through the window. The sky wasn't clear. There were a few hazy banks of cloud.

"What do you mean?" he heard himself asking. He was overwhelmed by his inability to understand her.

"Mum says I have to stay away from you, that you're no good."

"People say lots of things that aren't true."

"But maybe you're just like the others."

"Who?"

"The people from child welfare and that."

"I don't know anyone from child welfare."

"Are you going to report me?"

"What do you mean?"

"To child welfare."

"Of course not."

Now she was quiet again and hanging her head. She picked at the broken trim of her flip-flop.

He went into the bathroom, stood at the mirror, looked at himself and said, "Send her away. You can't deal with this too."

But he couldn't shake the image of the girl turning slowly and smiling up at him. She'd asked it to test him. He should have realized that straight away. Now of all times, he needed to show who he was. That he was more than an ex-prisoner, a number on the roll in the courtroom, a percentage in the psychologist's statistics.

He opened his eyes wide and forced himself to look his own reflection in the eyes. "I'm honest," he said. "I'm good. I can take care of her." And, as if she was standing there next to him: "You're safe with me. It's late now. You have to go, but tomorrow I'll show you that you can trust me." He thought back to the healing calm she had radiated, ran the water over his wrists and went to rejoin her.

"It's gone half-three," he said, and heard that his voice was still tight. He glanced at the alarm clock, whose hands were advancing silently and imperturbably. "It's getting late. I still have to clean and cook tea for my mother."

She'd undone her ponytail again and was fiddling with the hairband. She looked at him with a slight smile, but he could see that her eyes were dull.

"Are you hungry too, maybe?" he blurted, as if someone else had forced it out of him. She nodded, slightly embarrassed, then looked up at him with a sideways glance.

"Have you got anything yummy?"

"You'll see," he said. "I'll get something for you. But my mother's asleep, so you have to be really quiet. You're not allowed to make any noise."

She nodded.

Ten more minutes, he thought. He'd promised to wake his mother up at four. But he couldn't send her home hungry. There was a pounding in his forehead. He looked down at his feet. It was a good thing he'd taken his boots off downstairs. Very quietly he slipped downstairs in his socks, his neck muscles tense.

Less than five minutes later he was back with a plate of pollock and mash he'd warmed up in the frying pan. The girl was where he'd left her, kneeling in front of the aquarium, watching the fish.

He put the plate down on the floor, filled cups of water for himself and the child, fed the fish and sat down next to her. Listening to her eat, he stared at the downy hair on the back of her neck. Within arm's reach. But that was possible now, with him doing so well. Minuscule blonde hairs he wanted to feel against his cheek. Through the open window he again heard the quiet scratching of birds' claws in the roof gutter and, a little later, fluttering as the pigeons flew off.

You help me with the fish and the dog, he told her in his thoughts. I'll help you with food and company. He felt his blood glowing. She understood him. And he understood her. This could go well. It wasn't the same as last time. This, he could manage.

JONATHAN AND HIS MOTHER were in the kitchen by the half-open window. The fan was on. They were sitting across from each other and his mother was shuffling the cards. While he was waiting, Jonathan thought about the girl. He'd seen her again this afternoon after work. Yesterday he'd adjusted his daily schedule slightly, marking the period from three to four as "free" time. His mother wanted to have a nap in the afternoon and he needed to relax more. He'd been finding the days tiring, especially in the unremitting heat. This afternoon he'd sat on the square with the girl and the dog; after that he'd had some sandwiches with his mother, who now wanted to play cards.

He thought about how it had gone that day. Showering after work, he'd fretted about whether he was being productive enough at the factory. Despite the air-conditioning, the heat seemed to slow him down there too. But the instant he saw the girl on the square those worries vanished: there was only the moment, the two of them together, everything around them shut out by the solid block of heat, and now he wondered if that was a good thing. Maybe. Inside his body it had stayed quiet. He thought about the way she'd talked about the animal club. The light that splashed up out of her eyes. Her voice. Her lips. All the vowels and consonants that sounded so beautiful and round in her mouth, like little pebbles. He tensed his fingers and then stretched them, joint by joint. The cracking of his knuckles.

What were the exact words she'd used? What precisely had she said? He should have written it down. Trying to retrieve it now, it was like his thoughts were breaking up, dissolving, leaking out of him. There was a hole in his memory, at least it felt like it. But this afternoon it had gone well, that was the most important thing. It *had* gone well, *hadn't* it? he asked himself again. Yes, he thought, it had gone well. The way she'd stood before him. He'd noticed faint sweat stains around the neck of her top, but her smell, that vague, pleasant tang of perspiration, hadn't come too close. Only his fingers, quivering slightly, nothing else.

"Isn't it lovely, being able to do this together again?" his mother asked as she passed him the cards.

He nodded and felt like he should assent more forcefully, but he was so preoccupied with his thoughts and the heat that he could only scan the room from under his lowered eyelids, as if searching for a way to keep cool. His eyelids were damp. He couldn't remember it ever being so warm. And the day just dragged. Looking at the clock for a moment, he saw the long hand moving forward in little spurts—quarter to seven. He waited for fourteen minutes to, just to see time change, to convince himself that not everything was completely static.

The sun was still shining in through the window, burning hot. He slid his chair back from the table, away from the window, and angled his head away from its rays, though he knew it wouldn't help. He felt dehydrated, his eyes were stinging and his tongue was swollen and sticky.

It was like his mother could tell. "Shall we have another drink?" she asked. "Could you get me another wine? And a beer for yourself, maybe? Nice and cold?"

No alcohol. The text in the workbook lit up inside his head. Under the influence of intoxicants you could lose your inhibitions. If you drank there was a higher chance of doing things you didn't want to do. Bad things.

"So, you going to get something?" he heard her ask.

He looked up and smiled. "Sorry. On my way." She smiled back at him.

Despite the scorching heat and his clammy hands, he felt a strange, calm satisfaction. Maybe a drink wasn't that bad, he thought. Just one. What could go wrong? The girl wasn't even here. Besides, he had worked so hard the last ten days, he deserved it. That might not have been a correct thought, he interrupted himself, and for a moment he wondered if this was what the workbook called "cognitive justification". Or was he getting two terms mixed up? It definitely said something about justifications and there was something with cognitive, actually loads of things with that word, but he couldn't remember what exactly they were. His head started to glow. He'd look it up in a minute. Just don't think about it, he hushed himself. One drink won't do you any harm. A little drink will actually relax you.

In the kitchen he searched the cutlery drawer and cupboards and finally found an opener printed with the name of the supermarket round the corner. He unscrewed the lid of the wine bottle and took a bottle of beer out of the fridge. It had been there for months and the beer wasn't fizzy enough to make a proper head, but it was cold and he knew it would taste fantastic; it had been so long since he'd had any.

Jonathan and his mother clinked glasses without a word. She smiled and he smiled back, but still felt like he needed to say something. He mumbled "Cheers" and it sounded strange to him, awkward. He wanted to try again and repeated it, "Cheers," a little louder this time and now she too said, "Cheers. Lovely, son." She dealt.

The bitter beer tingled faintly on his tongue and cooled his mouth. Almost immediately the alcohol went to his head and he noticed his muscles relaxing. A mist rose between him and his thoughts like a protective haze. He leant back, the wickerwork of the chair creaking softly. Things were going well.

"Jon," he heard her say after a while. "Your turn."

The cards in his hand were soft, warm and smooth. Half-faded pictures: jack, queen, six of clubs. No ace, no joker. He never got aces. He'd had a pack in his cell too, sent by his mother, but he hadn't played a single game. Sometimes he did shuffle them before spreading the cards out evenly on the table in front of him, then picking one by random just to see what it was, as if that would somehow reveal what fate had in store for him. But he'd never been able to discern any meaning or pattern.

"Goodness, it's getting exciting," she said. "You're taking so long, I'm getting very curious…"

For a moment he took in the look on his mother's face. That teasing smile and expectant expression: he saw them often when they were playing cards together. He searched her features, listening to the ticking of the clock and the television noise from the living room. Unwanted thoughts began blowing through his mind. Suddenly he wondered if she'd noticed that the girl had been here a couple of days earlier. Or that he'd sat out on the square with her that afternoon.

And if she knew, what did she make of it? He studied her. The way she was bending over the cards, her small, weary face, her grey hair. Her crumpled collar and restless fingers. For a second he felt like he'd swallowed a handful of earth and couldn't get it out of his throat. What right did he have to disappoint her so badly? If things had turned out differently with the evidence in court, she would have been alone for a very long time. He could never let that happen again. But it wasn't going to happen again—did he need to tell her that, explaining that this was different?

A ship's horn in the distance distracted him and he returned his attention to the cards, picking out a few. He put on a bright expression and laid them out.

"Oh, that's an easy one," she chuckled, using the tone of voice she always adopted when she thought she was about to thrash him.

"Just you wait," he replied, laughing along. He tried to block out the strange mixture of ease and agitation he always felt during their games. Familiar yet painful.

Neither of them spoke. It was quiet for a while. She was thinking, letting the chain of her necklace glide quickly through her fingers. He heard her drink, swallow, breathe. Quietly he chewed the inside of his cheek. I'm a good son, he told himself. I clean. I cook as well as anyone. I play cards with my mother. But at the same time he pictured her sitting here alone at the table for all those months, under the bare bulb that gave off a pale, hard light in the wintry dark. She dabbed her face and throat with her hankie. They played on until the outside light began to fade. She won three times.

Towards eight, when it was almost time for him to take Milk out for a walk before doing the exercise he'd neglected that afternoon, his mother said, "Come on, I'll show you where we're going to be living. The letter from the council arrived. There are still a few empty houses."

She stood up, got a map of the new estate out of the kitchen cupboard, spread it out on the table and took some time to smooth it out with both hands. Now she was leaning over the table, he saw once again how small she was, so much smaller than him.

"Look," she said, "there's still three vacant houses in Rogstraat." She tapped the map with her nail. "If we move into number 47, we'll be right on the corner, next to the garage, then we won't have anyone next door. If we take number 12 we'll have neighbours on both sides. We get to choose."

Deep in thought, she stared at the map. He only glanced at it. The change, the adaptation that would soon be required of him didn't bear thinking about. He knew it would take months before he felt comfortable again. His gaze moved between his hands, motionless on the tabletop, and the crucifix he had once nailed to the door frame. Next to Mary, her eternally dying son, whose feet too were carefully dusted every single day. Sometimes he heard his mother quietly whispering to the statue while she was at it.

Once, just before he was arrested, he'd walked into the kitchen and found her standing in front of the statue with her eyes closed and her hands pressed together, saying, "Oh, Holy Mary, forgive us, let us..." He couldn't make out the rest. Silent tears rolled down her cheeks. He crept away before she heard him.

He only did a quick circuit with the dog. His footsteps were dancing; he was feeling light-headed from the beer. But he was still on schedule. He decided to get started with packing the first boxes. His planning was tight; he had to do it right away, then he'd still have enough time for his exercise.

He began with the cellar. As the alcoholic haze in his head slowly cleared, he removed piles of rubbish bags, cigar boxes and shoeboxes from the shelves. Old hymnals and exercise books full of songs from when his mother was still a member of the fisherwomen's choir. Letters from him he preferred not to revisit. Two old Bibles. He quickly leafed through them, just to hear the yellowed pages rustle under his fingers. He kept at it until he'd filled four boxes; the sweat crept up under his hairline, causing an itch he couldn't scratch away. He estimated that at four boxes a day he'd be finished next week.

In the slowly extinguishing daylight, he stood by the upstairs window and looked down into the neighbours' yard. It was empty. The space hopper was gone. Gradually the light changed colour. He watched pigeons take off, flutter around and land again as they searched for somewhere to spend the night. There were a couple hunched over in the gutter with their heads bent forward under their feathers. It was already ten o'clock when he walked back to his table. He wanted to do another exercise, but the beer had worn him out and he could only leaf through the workbook listlessly, trying to find where he was up to. His mind was a blur.

He sat down in front of the aquarium and looked at the fish. Tonight's exercise was about emotions. He had to fill in four words for anger in order of intensity. Irritation was the first—they provided that in the book, but he had to come up with the others himself.

"Do you know one?" he asked the fish. It stared past him for a long time and then, hardly opening its mouth, released a stream of bubbles with a weary sigh. As if it was trying to tell him something. Jonathan crept closer to the tank and studied its round, bulbous head. He saw the slow movement of its gills. It floated motionless in the water for a moment, then tensed its body and turned away, its swishing tail towards Jonathan. This isn't going to work out, he told himself. He stood up, flicked the dust off the legs of his jeans and felt a gust of warm air from the window brush over his skin. It was no good. It was much too hot to think anyway. He'd just have to do an extra exercise tomorrow. He made a new calculation in his exercise book: one extra tomorrow would be enough to get him back on schedule.

He sat down on the side of the bed, pulled off his jeans and peeled his drenched T-shirt off his body. For a moment he could smell himself. A heavy, dark smell. He then stretched out on his back on the mattress, whose springs creaked under his weight. The sun had set, but it wasn't dark yet. He fell asleep almost immediately, but not for long. When he woke up there was still a narrow band of light over the rooftops.

He shot up but didn't make a sound, his whole body tense. His heart was a dull pounding in his throat. The shreds of a dream were still stuck to the back of his eyes. Betsy. He'd dreamt about Betsy. He couldn't summon up just what he'd seen, but the short, high-pitched sounds the child had made were still floating around in his head. First cooing laughter that changed into an unbearable, short, almost bestial whine. Then the silence before she started crying. "Mummy, I want my Mummy…"

The pressure of his memories of her was building and the tears welling up in the swollen corners of his eyes seemed to be coming from a place inside him that had been covered over for a long time. Now torn open by the storm of images in his dream. Why now? he asked himself, but it was like he was asking someone else. He took his head in his hands and pressed hard on his temples with his index and middle fingers.

He wanted to curse himself, to hit himself in the face in front of the mirror, slapping his cheeks as if they were some-one else's. But he thought about the self-image exercise. It was important for him to go easy on himself, be mild, that was what he'd learnt. But how, how were you supposed to do that? The thought of reaching for the workbook was too much for him.

Let it go for now, he told himself quietly, and straightened his back. There's nothing you can do about it. Next time it will be better. He wrapped his arms around his legs and pulled his knees up against his chest. Again that animal smell from his own body. But he still couldn't stop the train of thought from starting off again, building up steam and rattling along on its creaking, worn-out tracks.

How could he have let it happen? He thought about the moments immediately before, before the offence, as they'd called it in court. He had been the same person then as he was now, he thought, what else, but he was still completely different. They'd looked for shells, razor clams and cockles. Folded them up in his green-checked hankie. He'd brought squash with him. They drank it together straight from the bottle, in the shade of a pine with long radiating branches.

He'd spread their finds out again, praising them and telling her about them. She'd stared at them in admiration before stepping over to him and kissing him on the cheek. "Beautiful," she whispered. At first he didn't budge. But her face was so close to his. And she gave him another kiss, patted the dog on the top of his head and went to sit down closer to him. Up against his crotch. Never before had he had a soft creature like her so close to him. She was so light.

The judge had ruled that he had abused her. But for him it was like there was something big, immeasurable, something unspeakable outside him that had abused *him*. That was something he would never be able to explain or even put into words. But there was something that had suddenly weighed down that incredible lightness he had felt inside him, just like that, without his being involved, behind his back. He had never been able to tell the psychologist—he would have thought he was a justifier, that he was "externalizing", as they called it, that he wasn't taking responsibility for his actions. But that was still exactly how he'd experienced it. How could that be bad?

He didn't have an answer and he shrank, hung his head against his chest and forced himself to stop thinking about it. "Now," he said out loud. "Now." He had to focus on the present. Everything was different now. He was different from how he'd been then and this girl was different too. Again he thought about how calm he'd been in her presence. He'd never experienced anything like it before. His getting to know her was actually a blessing. As long as he didn't get too close to her, he could practise. And wasn't that the very thing he needed to do?

When he was standing at the window again a little later, he saw the girl appear in her yard. For a moment he was disturbed by her being up so late, but that thought was soon displaced by what he saw. She was wearing a skirt. It was the first time he'd seen her in a skirt. She was tossing a tennis ball high against the wall. Every time the ball bounced back, she'd spin around quickly and clap her hands before catching it. With each spin he caught a glimpse of her thighs. His hands gripped the windowsill, the blood drained out of his knuckles. Yes, this was a good exercise. He could train himself like this. You could know everything in theory, he reasoned, and do exercises until you dropped, but in the end, you had to apply it. You had to know what to do in practice. So he kept on watching. The whirling of her skirt, her thighs in the glow of the dim outdoor lights, and still he managed to stay calm. As if the glass separating them was also a protective wall between his thoughts and his body.

After watching for a while, he noticed something else. She seemed to look lost. But before he could think about that, she suddenly stopped throwing the ball—as if someone had given her a signal—turned and disappeared into the house.

"She's alone," he told the tench. He sat in front of the tank for a while. The fish let a bubble escape from its half-open mouth and stared past him, as always. The blades of the fan were turning slowly and casting weird, warping shadows over the glass. "She wants to be with us," he said. In reply, the fish fluttered its pelvic fins almost imperceptibly and sank deeper into the mud. Its eyes were dull. We're all tired, he thought.

"She doesn't have anyone," her wrote in the back of his exercise book. And, under it: "I'll let her in. Tomorrow at three o'clock, when my mother's asleep."

He sat down at his table and did a self-control exercise. It went well. Then he stood up and looked out of the dark window. The tennis ball was lying on the paving stones. He walked back to the table, read a few more lines, then closed the exercise book and sat there for a while, holding it. Finally, he slipped it under his pillow, undressed and got into bed.

He'd fallen asleep easily, but woke up with a shock a couple of hours later from a dream about prison. The loud, echoing voices coming closer, radio music, the distant yelling of men in the yard. Footsteps in the corridor. He imagined himself shouting, his mouth as far open as it would go, but no sound came out; nobody heard him. Then that dry click—his cell door opening. The pressure of another body on his, wrestling, heat on the back of his neck, an arm around his throat. He had to break free of his dream, but couldn't calm his thoughts.

For hours he lay stretched out on his bed, staring at the ceiling, listening to the water pump. He tried his breathing exercises, and again, but only calmed down when he thought the girl into the scenario. She was sitting in a corner of the room with her legs crossed, just in front of the aquarium. She was breathing quietly and it was like the air streaming in and out of her lungs was trembling gently through the room. His own breathing now adopted the right rhythm too—in, out, in, out—and she just sat there in front of the tank. That was a sign. He was sure of it: the best thing was to let her in. He took his exercise book and wrote at the bottom: "When inside, she must maintain a distance of two metres."

"LOOK." She had her exercise book with her. On the front she'd written "PRIVAT!!" in big block letters. The spelling mistake warmed his heart. On the inside cover it said "The Club." It was Wednesday afternoon and they were in his room; she came over and stood in front of him. He saw that she'd written the names of the members on the first pages in felt-tip. With numbers next to them: "1. Tinca, 2. Milk", and under that: "Me". She said, "I think I can put you there too."

Jonathan flared his nostrils and straightened his back. He'd given his plan a lot of thought and written it out neatly. He'd adjusted his daily schedule. She could come from three to four. With the weather this hot, his mother had an afternoon nap every day at three o'clock and he woke her up again an hour later. The girl was always out on the square around three. If he passed by with the dog he only needed to call her and she'd come with him right away, he'd noticed that. He saw it all before him. Them, cleaning the aquarium together. Her, happy and laughing again, grateful. All thanks to him.

Just then, when he suggested she come with him to help with the fish, she'd jumped up from the game she was playing. She had a doll lying on the paving stones and a length of clothes line tied to a lamp post as a skipping rope, and had been turning the cord lethargically.

She'd followed him in past the living room where his mother was asleep on the sofa and quietly climbed the steps, all thirteen of them.

"Look," she said again.

"Yes, I'm looking."

She flicked through to the page about Tinca, where she'd written down all the facts he'd told her in small, neat handwriting. "Latin name: *Tinca tinca*. Real name: tench. Or: doctor fish. Does not like it hot. 18 degrees is the best. More than 23 degrees is very bad, hard for the fish."

He could hardly believe his eyes. All those details—she must have a really good memory. Just like him. As if there was a computer chip in there, hidden somewhere in the wiring of her brain.

"Did you just remember all of that?"

"Sure." Her face at an angle, her hair in that cropped, crazy ponytail. Now she was smiling at him, revealing her broken front tooth. The sharp, chipped corner, the tip of her tongue resting on her lower lip.

He could tell she looked up to him. Light sparkling in her eyes, minuscule droplets on the bridge of her nose. As if to draw attention to them, she puckered her nose a couple of times, just for an instant, a wrinkling, a quiver of her nostrils. "I had a dream about Tinca last night," she said. Immediately his own dream popped into his thoughts. Did she have that too? Dreaming so vividly that she still saw the colourful, moving images before her in the morning? He would have liked to tell her about his dreams, but couldn't think of any that were appropriate. Last night's, the one about Betsy, definitely wasn't.

"What did you dream?" he asked.

"She was sick."

He looked at her face from the side. She sighed. He thought he could detect fear, but he wasn't sure. Should he ask her? If she was scared? Again he thought of his psychological assessment. According to the psychologist he wasn't good at recognizing other people's emotions. And when he wasn't sure, he shouldn't guess: he should ask. That was a way of learning more about how people worked. But was it necessary now? He frowned. His stomach started to rumble, as if he'd eaten something dodgy. What would happen if he asked her? Would she answer honestly? And if she really was scared, what should he do? He looked at her, engrossed in her exercise book. The moment had already passed; it was too late. He bit his lip and didn't speak. Her pen scratched over the paper.

After a few long minutes she started talking again. "Tinca isn't going to die, is she?"

"What do you mean?" Tell her something to reassure her, he thought, talk about facts, about the fish. That'll give you more time to think.

"Because it's more than 30 degrees. That's too hot. It's too hot for people too, that's what Mum says, she almost suffocates behind the bar." At those last words, she shook her head slightly, releasing a lock of hair from her ponytail. The wispy lock fell down over her forehead. She blew it away. Like always, it flopped back immediately.

"Not if we look after it properly," he said. "It won't die then." He had to think of the cichlids he'd had last year. From his mother's letters he knew that they'd all died during his very first week in jail. She'd put them downstairs in the living room. He figured they were too sensitive to change. I'll keep this fish here, he suddenly thought, changing its environment another time would be too much for it.

"Before, when I was sick, Dad would always make me ice lollies. Pear-flavoured. That's my favourite."

Together they looked at the tank with the fish swimming slowly behind the glass, heavy and sluggish, its tail gaunt, its eyes dull. A murmuring emptiness suddenly spread through Jonathan's head. The last few days the fish had spent almost all its time lying in the mud. Hardly touching its food. With this weather it was almost impossible to keep the temperature of the tank low enough. Losing the fish didn't bear thinking about. He'd be alone in the room again, alone with his thoughts. Talk, he thought, say something, anything, cover it up with words. "We just have to be nice to it," he managed. But a stream of anger was bubbling up inside him.

"What's her favourite food?"

"It likes snails."

"What, just ordinary snails?"

"No, water snails, the common bithynia."

"So we have to give them to her to save her?"

"Maybe."

"Where do they live?"

"In the ponds in the dunes."

"Have you got some here?"

"There's a few left."

"Then we have to go and get some more with the club."

He nodded. One of these days he'd have to go back into the dunes, but he knew she'd want to go with him. That was too dangerous. He decided to let it rest, and to distract her he said, "Hang on, you can feed it a couple now." He fetched the jam jar he kept the snails in out of the bathroom.

She sat down on the floor with the big round jar in her hands. "What funny snails," she laughed. She traced each snail's twisting movements on the glass with her index finger.

For a while he limited himself to sitting there quietly and studying her from the side, ready to jump up quickly if she made any unexpected movements or came too close. But she concentrated on the snails and didn't pay him any attention.

After watching her for a while, he was struck by the strange feeling that he was under observation. As if the judge and the psychologist could see him sitting there in his own bedroom. Look, he wanted to say, look how well it's going. He cleared his throat. "Just give it all of them," he said.

"You sure?"

When he nodded, she carefully extricated one snail from the tangle in the jar, raised it up above the tank between her thumb and index finger and dropped it in. A little ring formed in the water, smoothing over again almost immediately. While changing position, he realized that before he'd got to know the girl there had never been anyone else in his room apart from his mother. And that it was also the first time that someone had understood him so well and without words. He swallowed.

The snail was floating motionless in the water. For a moment the fish drifted just above the mud, steering with gentle movements of its tail, then rose up and slowly approached its prey, opening its jaws just wide enough to swallow it before sinking back down again.

"She ate it up!" she cried. "Did you see that?"

"You did that really well. Now it'll be sure to get stronger fast."

She smiled at him. Very cautiously he smiled back. He mustn't show his feelings too much. He stood up and moved further away from her with a couple of short steps, but she was already coming towards him again. Without knowing it, she left the circle he had drawn around her in his thoughts, but he still stayed where he was, concentrating on his tense breathing. She's crossed my boundary, but I can do it.

"Look." She was holding her exercise book under his nose. He smelt a vague smell of soap rising from her body.

He was shocked. Think. ABC: Activating Event. Your feelings don't need to lead to Consequences. And your Beliefs, rational or irrational, how did that go again? Why had it all escaped him now, just when it was so important? Just when his own thoughts were getting entangled, catching on each other, twisting into knots. And for a moment all of the air between the thoughts was sucked out and made way for an oppressive vacuum in his head. He had to get free.

"Are you hungry, maybe?" he asked to distract himself. His voice was so thin, a thread, an air bubble that would burst before anyone heard it. He coughed and tried again. "I could make you something to eat?" That was better. Mentally, he took a step away from her. In his pocket, he clenched his right fist.

She shrugged and pouted. "You didn't even look."

"I did."

"Here." She came even closer. "Look, this is you with Milk and Tinca." A drawing of the three of them. He felt like going up on tiptoes to get a bit further away from her.

"Nice," he said. "The fish especially. It looks just like it." He moved his gaze from the exercise book to the window. Watching the curtains moving very slightly in the breeze. Swaying slightly to and fro. Inside he was tottering. As if he might fall forward at any moment, tumbling down inside himself. Carefully, he moved his weight from his heel to the ball of his foot. You need to be alone, get your thoughts in order. He walked towards the door.

"Is your mother home this evening? She cooking for you?"

"She has to work. She won't get home until I'm asleep."

"Wait here, I'll make something for you. I'll be right back."

Standing at the stove, he warmed up last night's leftover fish. His hands were shaking. But there was also a kind of calmness inside him. Tensely he followed the rhythm of his breathing, slowly expanding waves that seemed OK. Things weren't going

quite the way he'd planned them—she'd come too close. He'd
smelt her. But despite the blood he could feel beating warmly in
his ears and the rapid pulse under his skin, he felt good about it.

He began to push the chunks of fish around the pan with
a fork, too impatient to wait for the butter to heat up properly,
and spread a couple out on two slices of bread. I forgot to
warm up the sauce, he thought, looking at the pan. It's OK
like this though. I'll give her some salad dressing to go with it.
He stood still for a moment. Emphatically, opening his mouth
wide, he took a deep breath. Then he talked to himself, forming
the words without making any sound. It's crucial that you stay
alert. Keep a close watch on everything, don't be distracted by
what she says, keep an eye on the time. Quarter to four, he read
on the oven clock. Get a move on.

A little later he was back upstairs with her, feeling calm but
watchful. She was eating quickly but respectably, cutting off
bite-sized pieces and using her knife and fork.

"Would you like some more bread?" he asked when she
was finished.

After giving it some thought, she shook her head, then sat
there quietly for a moment. Again he was surprised by how
gently peaceful it was in his room, even though she was there
with him. "Come on," he said, noticing that he had lowered
his voice, "we'll give Tinca some more to eat."

While he grabbed the feed, the girl crawled over to the tank.
She bent over it and accepted the pot from his hands. The glow
of the aquarium lights lit her throat, chin and lips from below.
He watched, tensed his back under his T-shirt and looked away.

"It's actually a bit sad that Tinca's been caught and has to
live here by herself in the aquarium," she said thoughtfully,

without taking her eyes off the fish. "If you're by yourself all day long, you get lonely and it hurts."

She sounded wise beyond her years, as if they were borrowed words, not her own.

"Who says that?"

"Dad." She looked around quickly as if somebody might catch her out. "He called yesterday. Mum had forgotten her phone and I answered it. He's alone." That look was back. Her eyes so big and bright. "He's not like everyone thinks. He's sorry."

He turned away and fiddled with the aquarium.

For a few seconds she didn't say anything else, then talked on, her voice so quiet. "He's sorry he wasn't nice to Mum. That he was mean to her. I think it's kind of sad for him."

He watched her from under his lowered eyelids. A part of him didn't want to know. But at the same time he could have listened to her for hours. He wanted to hear it all, how she thought, what she did, even stories about her family, as long as she kept talking and he could hear her words filling the emptiness of his room. His fingers gripped each other and pulled loose again, too nervous to stay still. He rubbed his hands together and pressed on his joints until the knuckles cracked. I have to do something, he thought, confused by how she sounded, what she'd said. Do something, anything, as long as it's something that's just for her. To make it up. Something seemed broken and he wanted to try to make it whole again. But how? He turned his hands palms up in a kind of apologetic gesture, reaching out to her and then pulling back—an insignificant movement.

"Where is he? Your dad?" Oh God, that too, why was he asking that? He was only making things worse. He chewed lightly on the inside of his cheek, on his lip, felt once again the slight trembling of his hands. Calm down now. Keep your thoughts under control. Don't ask. Cut it out.

"Where he always is, in our town. Mum wanted to get away from there." She sniffed. "Now he wants me to come back and live with him, but he doesn't know where we are."

He didn't want to look at her any more, but he did anyway. He looked at her eyes in the afternoon light, eyes that just kept getting more and more beautiful.

"You don't have to tell me about it," he said, whispering now.

"I *am* telling you."

Your voice is still too weak, he thought, and straightened his back. Self-confidence, he thought. Calm. You are the boss of your thoughts.

"Mum wants to go away—we've been here too long," she said. She started chewing on her thumbnail.

Now something started gnawing at the bottom of his stomach. Why was it all so complicated? Was it too complicated for him? Here you are, he thought, with all the things you've read, all the exercises you've done, and you don't have a clue what to do. Everything inside him had fallen silent. He suddenly felt an intense longing to escape the situation.

In the meantime, the girl had sat down next to Milk, who was asleep in the corner of the room, and started whispering to him. Jonathan couldn't hear what she was saying and didn't want to hear. He got up and walked past behind her and into the bathroom, trying to think. But his thoughts weren't cooperating. They weren't racing like they sometimes did, but jumping up and down on the spot. Sometimes they stopped for a moment and fell quiet, so that he could see them, but there were so many and he had no idea which ones to focus on, which ones were right. Send her away, leave her here, ask more questions, mind your own business.

Grab that workbook, quickly read some of it, no, don't, solve it your own way.

His own eyes looked back at him questioningly from the mirror. He turned on the tap and let the water trickle down his forearms, his wrists. Little droplets splashed into the washbasin, trying to escape, fleeing over the smooth porcelain, but irrevocably sliding down to form rivulets to the drain. You're halfway through your workbook, he reassured himself. Actually more than halfway. And it's going better and better. You mustn't forget that. Don't forget it, he whispered, exaggerating the movement of his lips. It can only get easier. Better.

"Hey, when are we going to look for those snails?" she called through the bathroom door.

He cleared his throat. "Shhh, a bit quieter. My mother's asleep. I'll just be a sec."

He found her back at the tank, mouthing words to the fish. He sat down a couple of metres away and thought about what to say. It was almost four o'clock, he saw. She should leave. Wringing his hands, he pondered how to get her out of the room without being mean.

But while he was still trying to get his thoughts together, she turned and broke the silence. "I don't think it's true, what Mum said."

"What?" He felt another hot flush passing through him. What was this leading to?

"I think you *are* nice." She was now looking him straight in the face, her eyes clear and serious. "You look after Tinca and Milk, don't you? And me? I think that was a really terrible thing for her to say."

His muscles tensed up again and his back straightened. He looked away from her, incapable of reacting. He knew what he did last year was bad, and ever since he'd wanted to know what it meant, what it said about him. He'd thought about it so much he had sometimes felt like he was driving himself mad with all those contradictory ideas, and now this.

She'd turned her back on him again. He looked at her, the beautiful, subtle curve of the back of her head, the gentle quiver of her ponytail. Was her saying this a good thing? Was it something he could be proud of? Was it maybe the very thing he should do? Be with her, he thought, look after her.

It actually seemed very logical to him. Like what he'd written in the psychologist's questionnaire where there were parts of sentences and you had to complete them. Things like "I am best at…" And he wrote: "I am best at… caring for other people." But only after giving it a lot of thought. Because it wasn't really something you could say about yourself, was it? He'd worried about it, chewing the end of his pen, walking from the table to the window and back, before finally deciding that it was allowed. And it was true.

He went back into the bathroom, drank some water, stood at the mirror and looked at his reflection. When he went back into his bedroom she was sitting on the floor with her legs spread wide, bent over her exercise book. There was a tiny stain in her crotch. He felt his gaze clamping onto it. The blood surged through his temples.

Five minutes late, according to the daily schedule, he and his mother were sitting in the living room watching yet another quiz show that didn't interest him. Today he'd brought cod from the factory and hastily fried it, peeling some potatoes and putting them on to boil. But because he'd done an exercise in the meantime he'd forgotten to watch the clock. The potatoes were soft and mushy and, to his fury, he had to bin them. Quickly he peeled some more and stayed in the kitchen while they boiled.

He just couldn't calm his head. There was so much to think about. He kept seeing the expression on the girl's face when he sent her away just after four. An hour later she was already ringing the doorbell to show him a drawing in her exercise book: a fish, the club logo. His mother, who had dozed off again, woke up and he saw her peering out through the curtains. He sent the girl back home.

He served tea at twenty-five to seven after opening the windows on both sides of the house. They ate on the sofa. The fan was blowing warm air into their faces, but it was all in vain. The heat in the room was heavy and immobile, there to stay. His lungs were throbbing. He was tired and knew his mother was too. Her face seemed smaller than usual. Faint shadows under her eyes.

He sat next to her for a while with a steaming plate on his lap. She ate slowly, slumped back on the sofa. He was drinking squash; she had wine. The sound of her laboured breathing was almost unbearable. He knew she needed to take more medicine in weather like this. He'd seen the pots and torn-open sachets on the side of the washbasin. Drowsiness was one of the side effects.

After the quiz show, he surfed through the channels without speaking. There wasn't a single programme worth watching. At ten to seven he started getting restless. Five to, three, two minutes to seven, and she still hadn't finished her tea. He had to do three exercises today and so far he'd only done one. How was he going to manage?

She'd stopped eating again and her cutlery was resting on the side of her plate. She looked at him and sucked on her inhaler. That rattling sound. As if she was sucking little balls up through a straw. After that there was just the sound of the TV. He got up from the sofa and thought once more about the girl, the way she'd pushed her lower jaw forward again today, something he'd seen her do before. The way she'd shown him the pages full of notes about Tinca.

"I'm going to be a vet," she said, and when he asked, "Weren't you going to be a writer?" she laughed and her laugh was different from the one he was used to, rolling through the room like a gently bouncing ball.

Don't think about her, he told himself. Later, upstairs, when you're back in your own room. But it was like his mother could see straight through him.

"That girl from next door was here, inside the house, wasn't she?" she asked. Her nostrils were trembling.

A wave of warm, murky nausea rose within him. He closed his eyes for a moment and tried to let it fade away, thinking in the meantime about what he could say to reassure her. Talk, he thought, talk. Say something. It wasn't the way she might be thinking. But how could he explain it? He could hardly claim that he himself didn't entirely understand what it was about the girl, how her company helped him. And how he helped her. Her being hungry, yes, that he could say. But that wasn't all, that would give a wrong impression. Her having to choose between her father and her mother. Needing a place, a home. But that too didn't add up to the wonder of it, the strangeness he couldn't pin down. He fidgeted on his chair, looking nervously at his mother.

"She's helping me look after the tench." He had to keep it simple, giving her something she could understand. But he felt his mouth drying out.

His mother took the cross on her necklace lightly between her thumb and index finger and gave it a quick rub with the tip of her thumb.

"It's really important for it to eat properly now, and to keep the temperature right and for that girl…" he began, intending it to sound respectful. It was so strange: talking about her, about them together, made him feel bigger, more important. But he still felt embarrassed saying these things to his mother. Meanwhile, he thought about the girl's throat, with its soft hollows. Again he slid back and forth, bent forward, slumped a little, making himself smaller.

"The water's not allowed to warm up to more than 23 degrees, but that's not always possible. It's not eating."

He could almost feel the glow of her skin on his fingertips, the heat of her body. Strips of sunlight fell into the room through the venetians; the dog walked to and fro over its own shadow and he tried to concentrate on a fly that had settled on the armrest of the sofa. He looked at the gossamer threads in its transparent wings and felt his face cramping.

"I understand that that girl likes coming here, son," he heard her saying. "With Milk, who she walked all this time, and now that beautiful fish."

He nodded. It was true. And she had no one.

"But, Jonny, she's a child."

He followed the progress of the fly, which had taken off and was now buzzing up and down in front of the blinds, searching for a way out of the room.

"Why don't you just give that club a try, son?" she asked. "People your own age? Who you can talk to?"

He closed his eyes. Maybe he needed to give her that much? Maybe it was the only thing he could do for her. Show his good will by signing up to the Bible club. How could she know about the methods he had learnt to find peace within himself? That was something he could never explain to her. The figures for repeat offenders. This therapy programme significantly lowers the percentage of repeat offenders, he said to himself, quoting the workbook. What had the psychologist said again? Thirty-three per cent less? Or was it 23 per cent or... Significantly lower, anyway. And that meant: a lot. How could he ever explain to her how it all worked?

"The meeting's Thursday, isn't it?" he asked, though he already knew.

"At four o'clock."

"That's tomorrow, after work."

She nodded.

"I'll go and check it out."

"That's all I'm asking."

He took the plates through to the kitchen while she changed channels again. In between washing-up, he pressed gently on his stiff neck muscles with his knuckles every now and then. An itch rose along his sweaty hairline and he had to think of the piece of scrap paper, the sheet of paper covered with writing he'd found just before he went to prison while cleaning her room, some Bible verses she'd copied out. Something about life being beyond your understanding and having to submit to the wisdom of God, and never being able to know another person completely. Some of it went over his head, but some things he did understand, and that bit about others being unknowable had stayed with him. Somehow he knew it was about him and it hurt. Every time he got a letter from her, it brought it back to him. No matter how much he wanted to, he couldn't forget it.

At ten past eight he took the dog out for a quick walk, came back and sat down again, wanting to spend some more time with her after all. He'd wanted to say that he'd be careful, but instead he asked if she wanted anything else. "No, thank you, son," she said. "It's sweet of you to ask."

It was half past eight. He had to keep going. Fill four boxes, the exercises. It was difficult. Today he cleared out the cabinets in his mother's bedroom. Everything he found annoyed him. Old bracelets she hadn't worn for years, a stopped watch, tarnished silver, empty medicine boxes. Why did she keep all this stuff?

At quarter to ten, too late, he was finally upstairs. Although he was three exercises behind, he wanted to have another look at an assignment from a couple of weeks ago. He felt confused. He didn't know if he was angry or sad, or something else. He couldn't hold them back, but what kind of tears were they? The exercise in the workbook said that he needed to be able to distinguish all of his emotions. But he had no idea which name went with the feeling he now had. He stared at the letters in front of him, which suddenly seemed much closer together, sometimes even bleeding into each other. There were so many. He sat there for minutes, staring hard at the words.

Then he walked to the bathroom, spat hard into the washbasin, filled a jug with water—after letting the tap run for a while first—and drank, but the feeling in his stomach wouldn't settle. He decided to repeat the exercise from all those days ago and tried to stay calm. Back in his room he leafed through the exercise book. He still felt sick; there was a heaviness in his stomach.

Finally, he found the exercise. And his answers. He saw his small, clumsy handwriting. A page of it, in four sections. Suddenly it all seemed silly. There were four basic emotions, it said: happiness, sadness, fear and anger. He'd had to come up with an example for each emotion. Something from his own life. For sadness he'd written: "When Mum's alone and I can't do anything to help." He crossed it out and started again. At first his head stayed empty, but then the thoughts slowly started joining up. Next to sadness he now wrote: "If the girl is unhappy and I can't give her anything." For happiness: "When she's

happy too and she smiles and I see her broken tooth glistening."
And: "When she gives snails to the fish and the fish eats them."
That was all he could come up with. Furious, he tore the pages
out of the workbook, screwed them up and threw them into
a corner of the room. Half an hour later he regretted it and
smoothed them out again, using paper clips to reattach them
where they belonged.

J ONATHAN LEFT straight after getting back from work and had to wait at the bus stop for a few minutes. He'd wanted to take his workbook with him to catch up on some exercises on the way, but had decided that wasn't a good idea because of the risk of others seeing what he was doing. He sat on the bench, picking at the bits of skin around his nails. A drop of blood welled up next to his thumbnail, a pinprick. He sucked it up, staring in the direction the bus would come from. He searched the cloudless sky for gulls but there wasn't a bird to be seen, as if they too were too exhausted to fly.

He'd looked it up exactly: the three-fifteen bus arrived in town at three twenty-four. Eight minutes' walk and he would reach the centre where the youth meetings were held just after half-three. The bus appeared on time and was already slowing down for the stop when he waved it on with a vague gesture, his face averted. The bus sped up again.

I'll take the next one, he thought. That's due at twenty-five past; then I'll get to the square at quarter to and be at the centre just before four. Still on time. He rested his hands on his lap, intertwined his fingers, then separated them again and studied the odd shadows his arms were casting on the sunlit road.

The next bus arrived at twenty-five past. This time he stood up, but even before the driver had time to slow down, he'd turned and walked off. He stopped a distance away and peered at the bench he'd just been sitting on. "I can't do it," he whispered.

The meeting would last until six, he knew that. The bus back left at seven minutes past six and reached the village at six twenty. That meant: home at half-six. Until then he wandered through the dunes, this time without the dog.

He thought about what to say later, when his mother asked him how it had gone. Carefully, as if something was holding him back, he tried to imagine that unavoidable moment, testing the words he had come up with, gently mumbling them with moving lips, even though he was saying them firmly in his imagination. He had to sound convincing. "It was good, Mum," or "interesting", or—what did you say when you came back from something like that? He couldn't think of anything appropriate. What it came down to was that he wasn't a good liar. And wasn't that one of his best qualities? He'd given that as one of his answers too, after "I am most satisfied…" Thoughtful and proud, he'd written: "…that I never lie".

At home he found his mother in the kitchen, where she'd started peeling the potatoes. She was sitting on a stool with the pan between her legs and pulling the knife back towards herself with short, nervous cuts. Her face looked overheated. She looked up at him with an expression that was expectant but tense at the same time. He was sweating in the heat and walked, after a cursory hello, straight to the fridge for a jug of water.

"It was really good," he said, facing the other way and with his head back to pour the water down his throat. "It was good." He didn't need to turn around to see the expression on her face, to know that she knew he was lying. But also that she wouldn't say anything about it.

L ooking out from under the sheets, Jonathan saw low clouds suffocating the gloomy grey sky. Six o'clock. For the first time he'd forgotten to set his alarm clock. He should have been awake ages ago. He sat up with a groan and swung his legs over the side of the bed. The springs squeaked wearily and creaked under his weight. He sat there for a while, rubbed his eyes with his knuckles and forced himself to focus on what he could see—his folding chair, the table, the aquarium—to convince himself he was really home.

He had slept feverishly and had an intensely realistic dream in which he was lying on the girl's warm naked body. He was in his cell and the girl was in his bed, slowly changing into Betsy and then back to herself. He was paralysed, his nerves severed, watching. An observer. He saw his own hand, his fingers, the way they pushed against her crotch, tugging at the elastic of her knickers and did what he had just managed to avoid doing to Betsy by quickly wanking over her instead, catching his come in his T-shirt just in time and pushing her face away, only realizing later that he had grazed her chin in the process. And it wasn't until it was much too late that he noticed her tear-stained face. And heard her "Mummy, Mummy, I want my Mummy." And he'd whispered "Sorry". "Sorry, sorry." She was sitting with her back against a tree, hunched over with her face strangely contorted.

He sat there motionless for minutes. Behind his eyes he felt a faint, gnawing pain. Eventually he turned his head and saw that the alarm clock already said seven minutes past six. He stood up and began slowly pacing. I have to go to work, he thought, but I can't get moving. He stopped in front of the tank and peered at the fish, which was floating lifelessly in the water. It had hardly moved in the last two days and was scarcely eating. He knew that tench could sink into apathy in hot weather, but this was so extreme he was starting to get seriously concerned.

Downstairs he went to the toilet for a long, unsatisfying pee, hardly daring to touch his dick, then made a sandwich in a fug of worry, cutting it into four equal pieces and eating it before forcing himself to go to work. Almost an hour late. Preparing himself for a reprimand, he walked past the small office with his head down. But the boss was busy on the phone and didn't even notice him.

He dragged himself through the morning and went out to wander around the harbour during his lunch break. Today he didn't have the concentration for reading. *Nature* stayed in his bag. He walked past the fish market and, after several short, restless bursts of staring at ships, carried on to the dyke behind the harbour. The abandoned shipping gear he always loved the sight of was scattered here and there, but today everything looked different. On the horizon vague mists were floating over the water. On the wharf there were traces of spilt fuel oil. Rolled-up rope with floats watching him like eyes.

He was looking for a spot where he could look out at the water and the few passing container ships without anyone seeing him, but almost immediately his thoughts returned to her. He saw her flesh: young, unspoilt, the undoubtedly soft spot where the curve of her bottom met the dimples of her lower back. He tried to resist but almost immediately had a hard-on. He looked around nervously. He couldn't go back to work like this. He scanned the deserted wharf. This was an emergency. He hurried around to the back of the fish market where it reeked of guts and offcuts, leant against the low wall and undid his fly. With trembling hands he pulled out his dick and closed his eyes, coming before he could change a thing about the picture in his head.

Ignoring the outside world, he trudged back to work, too tired to be angry at himself. It was so hot that even sounds were hardly carrying through the air. He heard his own breathing and the blood in his temples and even those sounds felt like they were coming from outside.

In the course of the afternoon he searched the pages of his exercise book for the telephone number of the therapy practice the psychologist had given him. "For people with the same kind of problems as you. You can go there voluntarily." Maybe that would be best. At the same time, he knew more than ever that he would never dare.

He waited until his mother had dozed off, then moved the telephone cabinet down the hall as far as the cable would go. A farce, he thought, and who for? Still, it felt important to at least act as if he might be considering it, to convince someone or something that he was serious about it.

Before typing in the number, he stood in front of the hall mirror for a moment, holding his exercise book. The face he was staring at was pale and tired. Vague shadows under his eyes. His skin was getting as dry as his mother's. The same kind of cracks were appearing at the corners of his mouth. He tried to see something in his eyes, an answer to the questions he felt but couldn't express. His face in the mirror was looking at him from very far away. Out of reach.

The telephone rang three times.

"De Waag, clinic for forensic psychiatry, can I help you?"
He didn't answer, listening to his own breathing.
"Hello? Hello?"

In the evening the fish was still motionless and drowsy in its lonely aquarium. Again it hadn't eaten. The flakes of dry food were floating untouched in the water. Half sunk into the mud, it had turned its back on him.

Maybe you haven't done things well after all, Jonathan, he thought. A few seconds passed in which he waited nervously for the fish to show some sign of life. It didn't. "Come on," he said, "turn around." Finally, the fish did turn its head slightly in his direction, only to turn away again immediately and resume its motionless floating in the mud, listing to one side. Tensely, Jonathan walked around to the other side of the tank and tapped on the glass to get its attention, to no avail.

In his thoughts he saw the girl standing before him with the look she'd had on her face when she was alone in the room with him. His hand slid down the inside of her thigh, he slid her knickers aside with his thumb. She kept looking up at him with a vague smile.

He sniffed, stood up, grabbed his head with both hands, squeezed his eyes shut and tried to think himself away from what he'd imagined. Think of something else. Now. Zoom out. Now he saw and felt himself. Dripping from head to toe. His wet boots, limp hands, broiled thoughts. Was this the end of the strength he'd felt in himself?

No, that couldn't be right; he was better than this. He needed to go by new daily rules. Include more rest. He sat back down at his table, his head pounding. The fan was moving the warm air around the room.

He looked at the panting dog on the floor next to him. Now and then he gave his coat a furious scratch with one hind leg. Tufts of hair would come loose and float aimlessly through the air around them. He sniffed. Animals had it easy. They were what they were. They only ever used their brains for the purposes for which they were intended: investigating the surroundings, estimating danger, finding their way. They didn't worry about what had happened or what might happen or whether they were good enough, or so worthless they should be punished or put down.

The itch came back. Shit. It was so hot he could hardly bear it. When was it going to stop? His throat was hot and burning and so were his armpits and crotch. He started scratching. But every time the itch lulled for a moment, it was only to flare up somewhere else. He twisted his shoulders, pushing them back against the chair, rubbing them on the hard wickerwork.

Now and then he felt sentences rising from somewhere far away, but before he could write them down they'd already dissolved into a kind of soup in his head, big sloppy lumps floating around each other. He turned the fan to a higher setting and tried again. A little later he draped a wet flannel over his forehead, but that was no help either. He leafed through to the next item.

"Don't give up," he read. If you couldn't manage to relax, it might mean that you weren't working hard enough. That you were suffering from internal blockages.

Suddenly he was furious again. As if it had a mind of its own, his hand tore the page out of the workbook, screwed it up and hurled it into a corner of the room. What did that book know about what he was going through, how hard he was working? What did they know about who he was? How could a method someone else had made up, a complete stranger, ever help him? He stood up, walked over to the bed and lay down.

He stretched out but was too hot and too angry to sleep. With his fists clenched he sat down in front of the aquarium. The water was trickling down his cheeks. The fish was in the mud with its back to him.

After a while he stood up again. In the bathroom he ran water over his hands and wrists, then put his head under the tap too. In no time he was hot again. It's no help, he thought. This heat is driving me crazy. If it wasn't this hot, everything would be better. But there was no sign of any let-up. And there was that noise too.

From downstairs the annoying voice of a TV presenter reached him in erratic, muffled bursts. "It's now or never... Go for it... Try your luck." That sound, he couldn't bear any more of that sound. He clamped his jaws shut.

He pushed the stiffened cotton-wool balls as deep into his ears as he could, but snatches of voices still got through. He got up, filled the jug and drank, letting the cool water wash through his mouth, past the back of his teeth, over the raw slab of his tongue. Waiting for it to glug down his throat. The wave of nausea now finally, very slowly, exhausted itself. He thought about her and waited until his insides had steadied and were calm again, like that Wednesday afternoon. He took a few more deep breaths. Then he unscrewed the cap of his pen, chewed on it for a moment, drew some lines in his exercise book with the ruler and wrote his new rules down one under the other:

> If she comes, she's only allowed in if my mother's
> asleep.
> She can stay until four, then we can look after the fish
> together.
> She can keep coming until the fish is better.
> If she's scared, I will protect her.

He didn't know just how he was going to do it, but it seemed right to him. Although he was writing intently, he felt himself growing tired and drowsy. It was so bright in his room. Angled needles of summer light were shining in through the curtains. He felt exhausted, as if he'd been working in the factory for days on end, and he began to drift off. His head grew heavy and suddenly slumped down to his chest. Immediately he shook himself awake: Pull yourself together. For a moment he fought against an urge to punch the wall. A little more, he told himself, come on, a little bit more. All right, then, he said to himself, but on the bed. With his back against the wall, he continued working. Five more good sentences. Five more. But after just three, his eyes started to roll and at four he fell asleep again.

He woke up with the workbook and exercise book on his chest. His chin on the pen. A stiff neck. He began to rub the aching muscles, but at the same time his other hand descended to his warm belly. He touched his dick, wrapped his fingers around it and felt that it was already half swollen. Immediately it started to grow. Images formed behind his closed eyes, appearing out of nowhere like the crests of waves, then disappearing under water again. The girl. The complete concentration when she'd looked at him with her soft lips and half-opened mouth. The images kept lighting up and dimming again. He could make them move: away from him and back again. Sometimes coming very close, sometimes staying further away, as if he could see them dancing, elegant and slow. He waited quietly, as if something was going to reveal itself. Approval.

Gradually a soft hum rose in his ears. He didn't know what it was, but it was quiet inside him now, a vast space, and nobody could see him. Everything around him and in him seemed inexplicably friendly and innocent, as if the world was on his side.

He let out a deep sigh. Gradually what he'd seen faded and he was floating motionless around a big, gently vibrating space.

Then, suddenly, he saw the towelling of her shorts stretched over her bottom. He reached for his stiff dick again, but pulled his hand back as if he'd burnt it. "Stop," he whispered to himself drowsily. "Don't." But he kept going. His breath was dragging through his nostrils. His warm fingers traced the course of his swollen veins. He began to move his hand to a slow rhythm. A little bit more, he thought. Just a bit longer. Think of something else. Empty your mind, just feel it. It was so good. A bit more. As long as he didn't think of her, it was OK.

"Sex is normal," it said in the workbook, "a normal drive." They had taught him that a better way of handling his sexual urges was to train his sexual fantasies. You had to replace unwanted sexual fantasies with others. Fantasies about women, adult women. It was all a question of learning and unlearning. Unlearning. Or learning and replacing. He repeated the words to himself a few times and tried it. But he couldn't think of any images that appealed to him and tried to think of nothing instead. His excitement trailed off.

Still, he persisted. It took a long time, but in the end he managed to come. Short and dissatisfying. After that he lay there for a long time, eyes closed, feeling the pumping of his heart, breathing heavily.

He raised his fingers to his mouth and bit down hard on his fingertips. You shouldn't have done it, he thought, not like that. It's not good. Not good enough. But, he countered as a feeble reassurance, it was better than this afternoon. He still had to change though. He opened his eyes and closed them again, too tired to think. He felt like he had to make something up to her, even though in the end her face had only been a blur in his imagination, just before he came.

Go to the bathroom, he thought. Go to the mirror. "Look at yourself," he whispered. He tried a few times to sit up on the bed, but sagged back down. If you don't do it, he threatened himself, you're doing an extra exercise as punishment. He didn't budge. He looked at the alarm clock. Thirteen minutes to ten. At twelve to you start moving. The clock's ticking seemed to speed up. At ten to ten he lowered his feet to the floor and went through to the bathroom, where he forced himself to look straight into the mirror and struggled not to start swearing at himself. Come on! With difficulty he opened his eyes wide and instructed himself to make a solemn oath. Holding two fingers in the air he looked at himself. "It will never happen again," he said, straightening his back. "Never again."

A little later he was back at the window with his hands on the sill and his forehead pressed against the glass, staring into the mysterious twilight. A blue glow that hid more than it revealed. It didn't look real, a screen that had been slid in front of something and could be pulled away with a single tug. Behind it, he thought, was the other world. The prison. You don't want to go back there, do you? He tried to imitate the prosecutor's stern, severe tones. Think what it was like.

He tried to imagine it again. How he'd spent hours wide awake at night, curled up on his side in bed. Voices on the other side of the wall. Dirty paedo! The attack in his cell that first week, three strong, the kick in the head, his neck bending back, his front teeth through his lip. But it all seemed so far away, like he was looking at it through the wrong end of a telescope. It was the first time he had even been touched by a man, ever felt those male smells at such close proximity, their body warmth, their fury. But the fear that had got hold of him there kept its distance now. You have to establish contact with your body, he thought—that was how the psychologist had put it. Inhabit your body. The relaxation exercises. Do the exercises.

He stretched out on his back on the bed, his hands once again clasped together on his stomach. He closed his eyes. "In through the nose," he said to himself, "out through the mouth." He repeated it ten times. But his breath stayed high in his throat and refused to calm down. Again. Once again he sucked air in through his nostrils as slowly as he could and held it, meanwhile massaging his groin where he could feel his pulse beating. After a while the girl suddenly appeared in his thoughts. This time sitting completely at ease in the corner of the room, patting Milk and quietly talking to him.

Immediately that strange, calming liquid flowed into his brain. Although it felt good, he ordered himself to think her away. He groaned and turned his head on his pillow, back and forth, pushing her image to the furthest edge of his imagination. But just before she went tumbling into darkness, he thought her back. Come on. "Come on," he now said out loud. In his thoughts he put her back in the corner of the room, chatting away quietly to Milk, feeding the fish. He stared at her back. Now his breath flowed out of his mouth in a long, even stream. Finally, he was going to bed calm.

J ONATHAN SAUNTERED through the deserted neighbourhood in his pool sandals, the dog following him. The sky was hazy and dusty; high up in the distance, seagulls were gliding away, everything slowed and curbed by the heat. The sea glittered and splashed softly against the wharf with its load of floating rubbish: boxes, plastic bottles, bits of nylon cord. All that light hurt his eyes, the pain expanding through his forehead. It stayed hot, seventeen days now. This morning at quarter past six, the mercury in the thermometer next to the kitchen window, above the empty geranium pot, already showed 26 degrees. By the time he got home from work in his overalls at half-two it was up to 34. He'd had a quick shower and pulled on some shorts.

Now he was walking to the square. He was expecting to see her sitting on the swing and there she was. One of the chains was broken and the board was hanging at an angle. He walked on, going a bit too close. In his mind he crossed the line he always drew around her, but right then he didn't care. He let himself be reassured by her face. She smiled. Her expression was as light as ever. Her eyes were big and interested. Above them, clouds were drifting slowly by. Alternating shadow, light, shadow on her face.

"Hi," she said. She was wearing those towelling shorts again. She stroked the ground with the half-detached plastic edge of her flip-flop. He saw scorched blades of grass, some gravel, sand and tenacious thistles that persisted in stubbornly reaching up to the sun. Always that hair on her neck, as light as down. She was rocking back and forth on that one chain in crooked, wobbly lines, with one hand holding the plank seat up and the other holding the book she was reading.

For a moment he'd considered turning around and slipping into the dunes through the back of the village, but he wanted to sit with her. He looked around. All of the houses on the square were gone. A bare, empty expanse.

He sat down on the bench, a couple of metres from the swing, a few steps away from her. This is good, he thought. I can sit here quietly. I can watch her reading. With her lips moving, like always. A very distant expression. Giggling twice at something. Now and then her mouth slowly drooped, and then she closed it again just as slowly. Today she was wearing a top he hadn't seen before, a sallow colour. It was too small for her; the material was tight under her arms.

I could look at her all afternoon, he thought to himself, and the light, the patches it made on the grass, the small shadows. It was very quiet and with her this close to him even the silence was gentle and mysterious.

"Did you bring something yummy for me?" she asked after a while.

"Maybe." Suddenly he felt like teasing her a little.

"What?"

He flashed the bag of crisps he'd brought, then hid it behind his back.

"What is it?" she insisted.

"Come and see."

She came over on her thin legs, which looked sticklike in those shorts. Her ponytail was messy, held together by an elastic hairband with big plastic balls on it. She kept having to push strands of hair back into it.

"Well?" she laughed. "What is it?" She wrapped her arms around him to grab the bag. A waft of her smell. Startled, he let go.

With a highly precise, endearing cautiousness, she pulled at the top of the bag with both hands to open it. A short, ripping noise. Then she started to eat. As fast as last time, but still neatly, taking the crisps out of the bag one at a time between her thumb and index finger. She stopped for a moment to squat down next to the dog, pat him and say something to him under her breath. Jonathan tried to make it out, but she was whispering too much. He slid forward and listened more closely. He still couldn't hear.

"Yuck," she said, puckering her forehead. "Now my hands are disgusting." And as if to check if it was true or not, she raised her hands to her face and sniffed her palms. She pulled a face.

"Here," he said, holding out a hand. She put the bag on it, without question, and he fed her the crisps one after the other. It felt like feeding an animal. A small, soft, foraging animal, he thought. Minutes passed and seemed to stretch on for ever.

"Will you push me?" she asked when she'd finished eating and had licked her lips clean with a few short swipes of her tongue.

He nodded and stood up, moving his head left and right, waiting for his neck to crack. He wrapped one hand loosely around the chain and supported the plank with the other. His hand now close to her bottom. He rocked her like that as best he could and gazed at the light shining through between the houses in the distance. Don't look at her, don't look at her neck, too close. A swarm of tiny flies quivered over the grass. From somewhere far away came the faint sound of a ship's horn.

The pushing lasted for ever. In the meantime, he kept thinking about an exercise he'd discovered. He'd noticed that he could erect a glass wall in his thoughts to block him off from his surroundings. So that no matter what was coming towards him he felt it less. With his eyes half-closed, blowing out deep sighs, his back tense, he tried to erect that wall. He only half managed. Every time he succeeded in putting the panel in place in his imagination, the glass started to vibrate and, slowly, wobbling gently, flowed away. He clamped his teeth together. The girl was humming a song.

He tried again and again the glass melted and flowed away. He bit his lip. Why can't I do it? I could a few days ago. It had gone well at the weekend. Why can't I manage it any more?

As if to test him, she half turned towards him, and started talking. "Mum thinks Dad's tracked us down. We're going to leave soon."

This made it even worse, much worse. His head pounded no. No, I can't listen to this now. I'm too tired, it's too hot, my eyes are swollen from the heat. Not this. Zoom out, he thought, look at yourself from a distance. That was another technique. Look at yourself like in a long shot in a movie. But his head was starting to spin. His legs were getting weak. Stop it, stop it.

"Dad asked me if I'd like to live with him. He rang up again. Mum doesn't know."

He tried to relax his muscles while keeping his eyes half closed against the shimmering light.

She looked up again.

Don't respond, he thought, and immediately rejected the idea. You have to say something. Don't think of yourself now, she's the one that matters, she needs to be OK. Now is the time, help her. Talk to her.

"What do *you* want to do?" he asked, then sniffed air in through his nose in little bursts.

She shrugged. "I have to decide. But I can't." She jumped up off the swing and went over to the dog. For a moment he was scared she was going to cry. Had he seen that right? Was her upper lip trembling? But before he could tell for sure, she'd looked away again, her mouth pressed into a thin line. With a closed expression, she kicked a few stray stones. The swing slipped out of his hands.

"If they find me they might send me to a home. Dad thinks Mum doesn't look after me properly."

You're staying here, he thought. Here. With me. And again he felt his heart in his throat. Its quivering beat. He asked, "Is that what your father says?"

"No. I just told you. He wants me to live with him. But Mum says we shouldn't put it off any more. That we have to move. Child welfare's looking for us."

Out of nowhere, an annoying squeak started in his head. A hand pushed him from behind, trying to knock him over, to make his knees buckle. He wanted to say something about the club—maybe that would cheer her up, make her feel safer. Maybe it would help. But what could he say? His arms, which just a minute ago were rocking her body, now hung limply by his side, his palms turned forward. His hands empty. Suddenly he felt anger rising inside him again. Despite all the trouble he'd gone to. Despite everything.

The girl bent over the dog, who raised himself on his front paws, stood for a moment with his snout trembling in the air and then, as if he'd changed his mind, sank back down to the ground. The tip of his tail moved very slightly. She stroked his ears, then straightened up again, sighed, sat down on the ground and started writing furiously in her exercise book.

He took a couple of steps towards her, as if getting closer would reveal the answer. Those boundaries were nonsense anyway, he thought. As if suddenly he wouldn't be able to control himself if he came within a metre of her. He'd change that in his workbook. Without thinking he turned his hands inward and covered his left wrist with his right hand, as if that was his vulnerable spot.

She lowered her pen and looked at him through her hair. There was something tense and furtive about her expression and her lower lip was protruding. After a while she asked quietly, "Will you help me?"

"What do you mean?"

"Well, if you want to join the club, you have to promise you'll always help me."

"Fine, I promise."

"You have to really promise."

"I promise."

"Do it then!"

"How?"

"You have to spit."

She jumped up. "Like this." With a serious face she made a *v* with her first two fingers, held them up to her mouth and pretended to spit through them.

"OK." He felt ridiculous going along with it so meekly, but he did it. When he looked back at her, she'd sat down again and had a slight smile on her face.

"Look." She pointed to a drawing she'd done in her exercise book with "Bythinia" written above it. Another spelling mistake. Thank goodness, he thought. That was a beautiful imperfection. One more. And for a moment it was like he could see his own imperfection gently reflected in her face. His muscles relaxed a little.

"What's that mean?"

"The name of the club, of course."

Before he could react, she'd gone off on another tangent. "And if we move, all the club members who can have to send each other letters."

He nodded, harder than he intended, but the thought of her going away and only being with him in letters was unbearable.

While she kept talking about the club, he watched her feet moving in her flip-flops, the way she kept curling and relaxing her toes and how the material of her shorts seemed to grow tighter around her thighs.

"There aren't any kids here at all. So it's only Tinca and Milk in the club. And you."

He bent over to pick a shell out of the soft, sandy indentation between two paving stones and put it in his pocket, where he gripped it tight. Something to hold on to. All at once he could have cried. How could he ever explain how beautiful she was? How he felt about her? What they had together?

"Look, these are the club's first rules!" From where she was sitting, she showed him the exercise book again. The first few pages were covered with writing. "Do you want to hear them?"

He nodded. Of course he wanted to hear them. He wanted to stay sitting here for ever. See time disappear, running away through the cracks between the paving stones. But he looked at his watch and saw that it was getting late. Almost quarter to four. When he'd left home it had just gone three. Time had caught up with him again.

"Quickly, then," he said, tapping his watch. "I have to get going." His heart was racing.

She crawled over to within a metre of him and sat down at an angle to get into his shade. She was breathing lightly and looked at him with what he took for a questioning, almost proud expression. She stared at her own words, paused for a moment and began. "Listen," she said in a solemn voice. She cleared her throat. "The members of the club have to be nice to each other all the time. They mustn't ever be mean. They're not allowed to push each other. They're not allowed to say that they stink. And if there are games, everyone's allowed to join in." She looked at him and continued: "They're also not allowed to swear, drink or shout. And when they're asleep they don't bother each other. At night they are not allowed to go into each other's rooms."

When she'd finished reading, she stared ahead for a long time, biting her lip and frowning. He felt the heat surrounding them.

He couldn't decide whether he should stand up now or wait a little longer, until she looked completely relaxed again, with a smooth forehead. He moved his feet awkwardly a couple of times and then jumped up. There was a rumbling in his head. A dark, rolling noise like thunder in the distance.

"Don't go," she said, standing up as well. She gave him that look again. "I don't know what to do. I want to be with Mum *and* Dad. But I want to stay with you too. I don't want to go away." She craned her neck, tilted her face a little and looked up at him with wide, bright eyes.

He could feel it in the pit of his stomach. Something inside his head was collapsing. Nothing, he thought. There was nothing he could do for her. He was helpless. He looked at her standing there. Her narrow shoulders and hips, her thin ankles. All of her. He felt proud to be together with her, but sad too. The skin of her arms, a slightly lighter strip on her wrist where she must have worn a bracelet or watch. He hadn't noticed it before and that felt terrible.

He wanted to leave, but couldn't get himself moving. And could he leave her in a state like this? Her eyes, he saw something in her eyes, the light, a gleam, the sparkle of moisture. But maybe it was all just the heat on the square. The afternoon heat, that scorching, unbearable heat.

"I have to go now," he said and heard how strange his own voice sounded.

"That's no fun," she said, pouting. She stood up and wobbled from one foot to the other.

"I have to cook," he said. "For my mother. And I need to feed the fish. And Milk too. Come on, Milky." His tense fingers ploughed through the dog's hair, which hung over his eyes in lank wisps. "Come on, boy, we're off." He smiled a pained smile. "But we'll see each other again tomorrow, won't we? That will take a lot of time to organize, going away, you'll see."

Now she came straight up to him and he held his breath, bottling the air up in his lungs. She raised a hand and touched him very briefly on the chest. He swallowed. It was between his breastbone and his shirt collar, which had a point of stiff fabric. Not so very far from the bone in his throat that was making it impossible for him to swallow, the bone whose name he didn't know and would never know. She moved the back of her hand over to his collar, gripped it and straightened it with a short, quick tug, as if he was the child, not her, and she said, "I think you're nice. I think you're *reaaallllly* nice."

At home he fled into his bathroom, pulled his belt open and wrung his hand down into his trousers. Furious, he started tugging and squeezing, squeezing hard. He squeezed until he couldn't bear the pain. Then his fingers slid down, feeling their way over his skin and he simply held himself. He began stroking softly and briefly did what he liked the most, but soon pulled his hand away again. And again that squeezing, even harder, even angrier. Then stroking again, caressing, pressing. Over and over. He wanted it and he didn't want it. He tugged harder and harder. Pressed his nails into his skin. Pictured her as he'd just seen her. Sitting in front of him: the back of her neck, her thighs, perfect, the shadow behind her knees, the hems of her shorts against her skin. His dick was so hard now. Part of him was still trying to hold it back, but his hands were moving of their own accord, faster and faster. Then he slowed down again, wanting to stop, but he had no choice. All his muscles were tensed. He closed his eyes, tears under his eyelids. Bastard, he said, why are you such a bastard? The tears stung. But it had to happen, there was no alternative. Again he accelerated his hand movements, tensed his jaw, holding on to the side of the washbasin with his left hand. Suddenly it went faster than expected. Images of her. Her half-open mouth, the stain on her shorts. A warm glow from the bottom of his backbone straight up to his head. He squeezed his eyes shut, shuddered a couple of times and then collapsed on the floor. He felt the tears coming.

He stayed there like that for a long time, with his back against the wall, slumped over, his hands wet with his nastiness and feeling more helpless than ever. Eyes closed. Not good, was all he could think. This is not good. Not good at all. He thought of the relaxation exercise and the exercises about protective factors, tension reduction. He'd done them all so faithfully. All those hours.

A muscle in his jaw started to tremble. He tried to calm it, pushing his lower jaw forward. More tears welled up but he held them back, wiping them away from the corners of his eyes with his sleeve. It didn't fail, he thought. It hasn't failed.

He couldn't let himself lose heart. Sex was normal, he told himself. You just had to replace the pictures, unlearn them, replace and…

But he couldn't follow his own train of thought. He couldn't remember it all and his body was so heavy. He pulled his legs up, wrapped his arms around them and leant over to one side, his head against the bottom of the washbasin. Calm down, calm down. His knuckles were pressing into his eye sockets.

Calm down. You just have to order your thoughts. It will be OK. You haven't done anything to her and you're not going to either. She doesn't have a clue. She's innocent—she'll stay innocent. He saw her eyes, her irises.

"Jon!" his mother called from downstairs. "Jon! Yoo-hoo!"

No, he said softly to himself. "No," he whispered. "Not now." He had to be alone, writing in his exercise book, thinking about what had happened.

"Jon!" she called again, a little louder.

Everything gone, he thought. Couldn't everything around him and in him just disappear. Sinking into the hole he so often found in his thoughts.

"Jon!" she called again, annoyed now. "Do you know what time it is?"

What if he didn't react? For a moment he felt like the rest of the world would not exist if he kept his eyes shut. That he could just keep sitting here with his arms around his legs and his hands clasped together, eyes shut, and wait until he had crumbled into little pieces. It wouldn't take long. Inside his head it had already started.

"Jon, hurry up!"

"Yes, I'm coming," he said now, but so quietly he knew she wouldn't hear him.

She'd come out of the living room and was now standing in the hall at the bottom of the stairs. Her voice was too close.

"I'll be there in a sec," he called, loud enough now. He rubbed his eyes for a while with the back of his hand, as if wiping away his thoughts, got up and gave his hands a long, thorough wash, face averted from the mirror. Now his horniness was gone, everything was different. He only found the girl sweet again and thought of her young face. The way she asked for crisps, with a little whistling sound at the end, as if she was trying not to show how much she wanted them. The way she talked. "*Tinca tinca.*" She liked to say it twice. It tinkled. He thought about how she'd walked away, her awkward ponytail, animal book in one hand, pen and exercise book in the other.

Suddenly he felt a stabbing pain in his stomach. A stomach ache. And he had to go downstairs, otherwise his mother would come and call him again.

Get up, he thought. Come on. You idiot. You can't help it. You're an idiot. But make up for it. You have to cook, clean, walk Milk. Early to bed. Do an extra exercise or two. Three. Redo them. Do all of the exercises all over again. Leaning on his elbows, he pushed himself up.

Vacantly, he mashed some potatoes into his gravy. It had been quiet for quite a long time. It was ten past seven and they were still sitting at the table.

He felt his mother watching him. Now and then she rested her knife and fork on the side of her plate to stare at him in an attempt to force him to look up at her. He avoided her and kept his gaze on his food as if it was nothing to do with him, as if he wasn't involved in anything, a complete outsider.

"Son, are you listening?"

For a moment his mother's voice raised him up out of the murky, formless thoughts he'd sunk into and he turned his head towards her.

"You're not going to make it like this."

"What do you mean?"

"The move. It's only five days now. These last few days you haven't done any packing at all." She shook her head, bit her lip, patted her eyes dry with her serviette and continued. "Just so you know, I'm not going to stay here. I can hardly breathe."

To emphasize her words, she took a deep but strangled breath. She looked at him from under half-lowered eyelids. "If necessary I'll pay someone to help me pack. We're leaving here no matter what. You understand that, don't you?"

He nodded without looking up, scarcely noticing how he was dragging his fork over a crack in the rim of his plate. The tines automatically followed the bumpy edges, scraping off coarse grit.

"And don't scratch like that."

He was completely gripped by an absurd hope that somewhere there was someone or something who could tell him what to do, who could give him a sign. It filled his head. Should he call that psychology clinic after all? Could they help him? Or would it only make things worse? He'd heard about that before. Them hearing from your voice that something was wrong, and then coming by or sending a probation officer after you. The girl had been at the door a few times in the last couple of days—should he stop letting her in? That no longer seemed possible. He couldn't even imagine getting through the days without her any more.

He tried with all his might to disentangle his thoughts and create a space in which he could assemble his sentences and answer his mother.

But suddenly she pushed her plate away and looked at him with her eyes wide and her nostrils flared. "Don't let that girl in any more and concentrate on what you have to do. If you keep this up, you won't leave me any choice."

Now he raised his head in fright. No, this isn't happening, was all he could think. This isn't happening. It's not possible. Not my mother. She's on my side. She would never report me, she would never betray me.

"I want to see you the way I've always seen you, as my dear sweet boy, but I don't know if that's possible."

Just then the dog barked and raised himself up on his long, unsteady legs. He stood for a moment, his hocks twisting. Jonathan looked at him, at his thin neck, his back, the bare spots in his coat. Scratches and bites where he'd tried to get at an itch; he was covered with those wounds, but Jonathan only noticed them now. They were shocking. What was strange though was that what he could see here before his eyes seemed much realer than what his mother had said. Whimpering quietly, the dog slowly lowered himself back down to the floor, reminding Jonathan of the fish upstairs, which was still floating half-dead in the tank and eating next to nothing. The graph of his weight had fallen under the one-kilo line; if that kept up much longer he'd soon be dead.

Jonathan was staring at his plate again and still hadn't said a word. His stomach felt as empty as it had before tea. But he had to go upstairs, and straight away. When he said so, his mother just looked at him without a word.

He withdrew to his room, closed the curtains and lay down on the narrow bed without pulling the sheet over himself. The fan was moving the warm air around and he thought of the girl again; her face was so small and familiar, right now she seemed more familiar than anything at all in this house, even his own mother. He longed for her presence, for her calming effect. He jumped up and looked out through the gap between the curtains, but the yard was empty.

He lowered himself down onto the floor. For a long time he sat staring at the water in the aquarium, wondering what he should do. Was it his duty to take the fish back to the pond? He could hardly bear to look at it any more; it was in such a state, and it was his fault that it was living here in such confined quarters.

But it was all too hard to understand and he couldn't decide what to do. Of course, it was his fault that the fish was floating here in his tank, but it had also been weak the first time he saw it. He was sure it wouldn't have survived in its natural environment without his help. He looked to see if he could discern any vitality or strength in the fins and the tail but there weren't any signs of life. No matter how hard he struggled to grasp what had happened, there was only room in his head for a single unyielding, stubborn thought. He couldn't take the fish back. Strangely enough, he felt that very strongly. It was like the two of them were facing a task they had to complete together. As if it wasn't just that his fate was linked to the fish, but as if the bond between them stood for something greater, something awesome he didn't really understand.

That night he hardly slept and in the morning he couldn't shrug off the feeling that everything was going in the wrong direction. He'd already decided that he was going to take a sickie and had sat up until long past three, bent over his workbook and trying hard to let the words sink in. At half-six the light woke him up. Tuesday. The sky was on fire again. The fish was floating half dead in the muddy water. Anxiously he studied the thermometer: 33 degrees. And the humidity was worse than ever. Breathing in, the air scalded his throat.

"Hey!" He tapped the glass with a fingernail. "Hey! Pull yourself together."

The fish hadn't eaten any of yesterday's dry food, which was turning into slush at the bottom of the tank. He lifted the fish out to weigh it, slipping it into the bucket on the hook of the scales. It didn't even resist. No more than 975 grams. He put it back in the tank and sat there fretting about it for a while.

Then he gave it some bread and some of Milk's dry dog food, which he cut down to size first, but it wouldn't eat.

When he'd finished changing the water in the aquarium and had scrubbed some algae out of the joins, he went downstairs to cook some sweetcorn in the kitchen, but his mother was already there, kneeling on a mat in front of the statue of Mary to pray. He hurried back upstairs and sat down again in front of the tank, peering into the thin, pale light. Then he stood up again to look into the girl's yard. Tomorrow. He had to let her in again, one more time.

He went back downstairs in his underwear and pool sandals. His mother was lying on the sofa and had fallen asleep again; a quiet, rasping snore was rising from her throat. He cooked some sweetcorn in the kitchen and took it upstairs. With what looked like a tremendous effort, the fish worked its way up to the surface and gulped at the sweetcorn before sinking back down to the depths again almost immediately. Jonathan knelt down in front of the glass and waited.

As if part of a sinister plan to break him, the letter he'd been dreading the whole time arrived from the public prosecutor's office around noon. He read that the case was being reopened. It said something about valid reasons for restarting the investigation, but he screwed the letter up before finishing it.

It didn't bear thinking about. In the hall he slumped down on the floor and tore the sheet of paper up into the smallest possible pieces, before sweeping them into a tidy little pile with his hands. Confetti, he thought. A tiny mound left over from a celebration. Even if there was nothing to celebrate. It was the very opposite. This letter announced the end of his life. Three steps from table to door, three steps back, a window, a locked door, fear. He was still squatting in the hall with his back to the wall. He felt the steady, ongoing beat of his heart and tried to think.

Somewhere inside there was still a part of him that wanted to act, to call his lawyer or do something, anything. But a mist had also formed in his head and was cutting him off. "Ring him up," he mumbled, thinking of his lawyer's blue tie. "Go on, ring him up. Get some help, you moron."

A copy of the letter had been sent to his lawyer. He'd start preparing the case immediately, looking for solutions and finding them. Wouldn't he? Surely? But Jonathan couldn't get his legs to walk.

Finally he made it upstairs and reached for his workbook, a few pages of which were coming loose from the binding. He leafed through it. Searching for his lawyer's number between the loose sheets with notes, the memory aids, the tension graph. But before he'd found it, he'd already lowered the workbook to his lap. There was no point.

It was over. He felt as if everything was already in place. He heard footsteps in the corridor that led to his cell block, the footsteps of big burly men. There were four of them, maybe five. But they were coming on behalf of more. They were coming on behalf of the whole ward, the whole hospital.

Jonathan pushed his fingers into his ears and put his head down between his knees because the racket, the threat, kept getting closer. Suddenly the terrifying horror of it all was closing in on him; the world was shutting off all escape routes. Someone had their hands around his neck and had started squeezing.

"Shhh, my mother's asleep," he said, nodding at her conspiratorially. He saw that she had her exercise book clamped under her arm again. "Sit down."

He went into the bathroom to get the scales. There was no question of not weighing the fish; even if he knew that it would weigh the same as it had this morning, he still wanted to do it again. When he came back into his room, she was standing next to the aquarium. Why hadn't she sat down? He started fiddling with the scales and felt her watching him as she hopped from one foot to the other, before following along behind him while he carried the fish, gleaming with little droplets of water, over to the scales, which turned to 975 grams. He quickly ran his fingers through his hair a couple of times in an attempt to stay calm. Idiot, he said to himself. What did you expect?

What was wrong with the fish? Was it just the heat or was it sick? He took hold of it and carefully felt its scales with his thumb and index finger, searching for lumps or irregularities. He pulled its lip out to look into its mouth. But he only saw pink, moist flesh, nothing unusual. All the time he could see the girl out of the corner of his eye, standing next to him, following his every move. She was agitated today and he was finding her hard to take.

After slipping the fish back into the water he noted its weight. The line of the weight graph had been going down for days and was approaching a level at which the fish was seriously underweight. On the opposite page he saw that it had been days since he had filled in his own graph, the tension graph. The last time, three days ago, it was at nine, the second-highest level. He didn't want to look at it and couldn't understand why the line just wouldn't go down again.

"What are we going to do now?" the girl asked, as curious as she was concerned.

"I'm almost ready, sit down." Again he looked at her. She was still jiggling from one foot to the other. She needed to calm down and do what he said. He tried to sound stricter. "I have to get something, just sit down."

He walked downstairs quietly—his mother was still asleep—filled a jug with ice water and carefully added it to the tank upstairs, one splash at a time, trying to cool it down. "Otherwise it's way too hot for you, isn't it, buddy?" he whispered. The fish swished its tail as if in answer, then sank back down into the mud.

Constantly aware of the child's presence, Jonathan leant over the tank, racking his brain about the fish and what to do. The girl had sat down for a moment but stood up again and came up close behind him, where she started talking. He felt rage building. Not now. Now he needed things quiet.

"We have to get some of those snails tomorrow."

"Sit down," he repeated and said, "give it some sweetcorn first." And then, "I've got some crisps for you."

Finally she did what he'd asked. She gave a serious nod. He passed her the feed and the crisps and briefly felt her hand, small and dry. Then he spent a long time wiping his own hands off on the cleaning cloth and took a few steps away before turning back to look her.

She was sitting cross-legged in front of the tank and frowning. Her eyes looked moist. Had she been crying? "Give Tinca a little more," he said to encourage her, forcing his face into a half-hearted smile. She picked a few chunks up out of the box and sprinkled them over the water, whispering to the fish while she was at it.

Together they watched in silence for a long time, waiting for the tench to start eating. But it stayed floating motionless a few centimetres above the bottom of the tank.

"We're leaving," she said suddenly. "Tomorrow."

His fingers curled. He wanted to pretend he hadn't heard, shutting it out, trying to raise a shield in his head that would deflect her words, but it was too late.

"What do you mean?"

"Mum says he knows where we are. We have to go."

The pain was back and moved into his stomach. But this pain was different and spread to his chest and made his windpipe feel soft, as if the cartilage was dissolving. He swallowed and made a few attempts to shake the feeling, but now it was like a fish bone caught at the back of his throat. His tear ducts filled. He closed his eyes, coughed a couple of times and felt something in his throat start to tremble.

"When?" His voice sounded teary, choked. Arsehole, he thought. Be a bloody man.

She turned away for a moment, then stood up and came over to him. "I don't want to go. I want to stay here with you."

He took a step away from her, sat down on his chair and before he knew what was happening, she'd plonked down on the floor right in front of him, less than an arm's length away. She pulled open the bag of crisps and poured them into the bowl he'd given her. He stared at her, so close. Tiny red flecks just under her hairline.

Suddenly he felt an unfathomable sorrow. About her leaving, about him being unable to escape any of it. Just when he might have found a good way of being with her. He didn't understand, and everything was spinning, as if someone had started to pull the rug out from under him with quick little tugs. He felt like he might topple forward at any moment.

She was sitting on the floor and eating the crisps a few at a time. He watched her eat, following her every movement. She wet the tips of her first two fingers and dipped up some crumbs. Then she crawled even closer and sat down again with his legs as a backrest. He could hear her chewing, swallowing.

Push her away, he thought, push her away, push her away. But he didn't do it. After sitting in confusion for a while, he looked down at her and saw how straight and tidy her hairline was under her ponytail, with very light down below it. Rapt, he followed the movements of her breathing under her top. She had never been this close before. His heart pounded in his chest. Her ear was very close too. He only had to raise a hand and he could trace its curve with a finger. On the inside his whole body was quivering. His back was sopping. From the other side of the room came the weary creak of the fan.

She sighed again. In that way she had. The way he found so beautiful. "Shall I read you a story I wrote?" Her voice was soft. Slowly she turned her head towards him.

"I think you have to go home."

She ignored him.

Without giving himself permission, he bent closer to her as she picked up the exercise book. The faintest trace of the smell of soap rose towards him. His body reacted immediately: a feeling that burned a path deep into his belly. His dick harder than ever. His throat constricted. With his eyes closed he listened to her every breath. Under his shirt his heart was going wild.

You have to go, you have to go, pounded through his head. He pushed her away from him for a moment, very carefully, but she resisted. She stayed sitting there, motionless, without taking her eyes off the page. Mumbling to herself the words she was about to read out loud.

"Once upon a time there was a girl," she began, but the words that followed didn't get through to him. He studied her bare foot in her flip-flop. If he lowered himself to the floor now and slid over a little, he would feel her against the side of his jeans, pressing lightly against him. Under the material his erection grew.

"And the girl also had a club," he heard her saying. "She wanted to stay in that club for ever. Everybody in the club was really nice."

His hands were trembling uncontrollably and he gripped the seat of his chair to keep them still. Under his shirt he was bathed in sweat. His mother would wake up any minute. She had to go. Everything was getting in a mess, his whole schedule. And while thinking that, he saw her get up. She walked over to his bed where the workbook was half hidden under his pillow. She reached for it. "Have you got a story too?"

"Hey, don't touch that."

She did anyway.

"Don't touch it!"

He strode over. He felt that he wanted to hurt her.

She held the book tight behind her back and looked at him with an expression he couldn't quite place.

"We have to go to the lakes early tomorrow morning."

"Give that back."

"My mother doesn't need to know. She's working in the cafe until late and then she'll sleep in. We're not leaving till afternoon.

He reached around her to grab the book but she stepped away. She obviously wasn't planning on going anywhere. In the same instant he saw himself pushing her over onto the floor with a shove of one arm and holding her down.

"It's so hot, maybe I can go for a paddle. You'll have to stay close, though, 'cause I can't swim."

He imagined holding her down on the ground with one hand, using the other to pull her shorts and knickers down over her thighs. It was unstoppable.

Suddenly she tossed the book back onto the bed. Then she undid her ponytail. She was just gathering her hair up again with the hairband in her mouth when he grabbed her by the arm. "You have to go now."

"Hey, that hurts!"

She turned and stared at him. For a second her eyes were as big and bright as ever. The copper fleck floating in one of them was a glittering splinter of glass. The sunlight shining in through the window was falling even more beautifully than before on her face, cheeks and throat.

A little later he was sitting at his table. He picked up his workbook and stared at the scratchy lines he'd drawn under the exercises, at the tension graph. Once he'd seen it as a system. How could he have believed that the exercises in the workbook could help him? That all those words, interconnections thought up by someone else, could have applied to him? All that effort had come to nothing.

Furious, he started to tear out the pages one by one, the pages he'd filled with his pathetic handwriting, that sad graph; with all his strength he pulled on them until the glue let go and those useless, stupid balls of paper started piling up on the floor. With both hands, he swept them together, wondering what to do with them, if there was any way he could possibly undo it all. All that wasted energy, all those hours he'd sat at his table, racking his brains, searching his body for answers. He thought of burning it, curling flames consuming the paper. Or he could shred it and flush it down the toilet as well as he could. He imagined himself moving, becoming active, flushing the paper away. But in reality he stood there and stared down at the pile, and in the end he didn't do a thing.

He thought about her unexpected movements, her mouth. Almost immediately afterwards, his thoughts went back to the therapy room. The psychologist was always talking about responsibility. But he *had* been responsible; he'd looked after her to the best of his ability. But she had still sealed his fate. He had nowhere left to go.

His gaze drifted over the room, lingering on the two packed boxes pushed up against the wall. It was his fault that they still hadn't left this shabby, run-down house. And he was to blame for the half-dead fish too. The hard time Betsy had had of it according to the other side's lawyer, his mother being alone again, and the new girl, everything that was going to happen to her—it was all his fault.

He sat down in front of the aquarium. It was boiling hot.

"I'm sorry," he whispered to the empty room around him. "I'm sorry." He kept his eyes on the fish. It had come up out of the mud and was close to the glass. Jonathan brought his face right up to the side of the tank and stared into its small, dull, orange eyes. A noise erupted from his throat. He wanted to bang the glass, but stayed motionless. He felt now as if even his thoughts weren't coming from his own brain, but bubbling up from a spring that belonged to him and his life, but was still completely foreign to him.

And the light was still there, leaden. He rubbed his eyes. He was so exhausted all he wanted to do was sleep for days. Fully dressed, he lay down on the bed on his stomach, his face hidden under his arms. He stayed like that for a while, dragging tired breaths in and out of his lungs, then turned onto his back and put his hands together on his chest. It was so light and so heavy at once inside his head that he felt like he only needed to close his eyes to sink into illuminating sleep. But he was wrong.

He covered his face with his hands, half opened his eyes under his spread fingers and watched through his lashes as the patches of light moved slowly over the ceiling. He tried to see himself from a distance. As if he was suspended there, wedged between the rafters, with his legs stretched out and looking down at his own body, his face hidden under his hands.

"Coward," he said out loud, but a different voice, somewhere at the back of his mind, also said, "You can't do anything about it." He felt tears welling up, made a fist of his right hand, then moved it from his eye to his lips, opened his mouth and bit his knuckles hard. "No," he said, "there's no point." Ignoring a thread of spit running down his chin, he stood up and leant on the wall. His neck muscles were so stiff the pain was radiating out to his shoulder blades and the base of his skull. From where he was sitting, he could see the light forcing its way into the room. The heat. Now he thought of that image of the girl here in his room, as he'd just seen her. He stared ahead, pressed his lips together, opened his eyes wider, let his gaze wander over the things in his room, then screwed his eyes back up and turned his gaze inward, but everything stayed far away.

It was over. He knew he was going to do something terrible. He'd never get out again. His breath was coming out of his nostrils in short, irregular bursts.

After pacing for a while, he went over to the window and waited till he saw her in the yard. His jaws clamped tightly together.

There she was, in her running shorts. The moment he saw her, he undid his jeans. He'd wanted to cry, but he wouldn't manage that now either. He stared at the child, the girl, the beautiful girl, who had her back turned to him and was bending over to unroll her skipping rope, whose cut and frayed ends he could now see better than ever. Slowly, with her back slightly curved, she walked from one side of the yard to the other. Five steps for him, seven for her. She put the doll down near the middle of the skipping rope and squatted next to that lifeless thing, her face close to its rigid plastic head.

The buckle of his belt started banging furiously against the radiator. He imagined her mouth moving, her lips forming words he, like always, could not make out. The tip of her flaxen ponytail was shaking very lightly back and forth. "There you are," he panted to the rhythm of his movements. "There you are…" His heart was pounding, fast and furious, but far away as well.

My life is over, ran through his mind at the same time. Over, he thought. His life was over before it had really begun and he didn't know for sure that that was such a bad thing. Or what it was that he would lose. It was all beyond him and he upped the pace.

The fish was dead. It was already slightly swollen, he now saw. This was what he had been scared of, what he had been worrying about all this time. Now that it had happened, he could only stare. It was floating on its back on the surface, pale belly up as if praying for help from on high, help that would never come. Scales hard and pointy, dorsal fins lit by the dim lights. He'd left the pump on all evening and listened to its quiet bubbling.

He closed his eyes to let the sound absorb him. This was something he was good at, disappearing. He began fiddling with the knobs, turning the pump up. Its drone still sounded quiet and constant, but the disappearance he'd hoped for didn't materialize. He rubbed his eyes and pressed his nose against the tank. He was so close to the glass the reflection of his face was strangely distorted.

"Look," he told himself. "That's you." But he couldn't manage to see through it, to get past his shadow: he was too scared and looked away. Then he sat there silently for a while, not moving at all, eyes shut and listening to the soft bubbling gurgle of air bubbles being blown through water. In his head the sounds were swaying dots of light, shooting through his mind together with the images.

When he opened his eyes he felt the tears. He knew that, however crazy it sounded, this was the end of him. Now that the fish was dead, he was done for too.

Before forcing himself to get up, Jonathan stayed lying on his back for a moment on the sweat-soaked mattress, eyes closed. He'd only slept in snatches, a few hours altogether, and was more exhausted than ever. His bones, sinews, muscles—everything hurt, everything was raw and strained. He tried to get up, but it hurt too much and almost immediately he lay down again, not even opening his eyes. It was already so hot that his whole body was covered with a clammy, itchy layer of moisture. The heat had penetrated into every part of his body, pushing him down on the bed, but in his head thoughts were in motion. With excitement as much as disgust, he watched them appearing like moving images of her being projected on a screen. Even after he'd opened his eyes and looked around the room, the images still imposed themselves on him.

She was sitting here in his bedroom, radiating warmth, almost shamelessly giving off her childish girl smells. He pressed his front teeth into his lip, slid over the mattress to the narrow dusty gap between the wall and the side of his bed and felt like tipping his body into it as if rolling it into a ravine, but there was no salvation. He slid back. Turned his head left and right on the pillow.

The soapy sweetness of her skin, the vague perspiration, even the slightly sour smell of her clothes. It all excited him.

He thought of her belly moving softly with each breath. Her bum, here on the mat, the way she sat there with her legs spread while he, while he just worked, and kept on doing his best, and now he wished he could come up with a way of explaining it that made it her fault too, some way, any way. If only he could make her partly to blame. He thought of her towelling shorts, how they crumpled around her crotch, the folds they formed, how underneath her bits must have those same folds. He was still biting his lip. He pressed his right incisor down hard but kept seeing flashes of her through the pain. And nowhere could he discover any blame in any of it, for all he wanted to. But he still couldn't see her the same way as before, as if some strange bond had been established between them. An agreement that had come into being without their involvement, as if a network of meaning stretched between him, her and everything around them, so that he felt it but couldn't push through to reach it.

He saw her from behind, as he'd so often seen her, but now everything seemed changed. She crawled towards the tank, like yesterday, but it was like she was being lit up by a different, strange light from outside. She was wearing her running shorts and the pale top that must have once been yellow. The piece of chalk in her back pocket, her short ponytail, her thighs, her ankles, her toes in her broken flip-flops. She didn't know what she was doing, what she was doing to him with her movements. But still. He saw her movements as lines, as gossamer threads tying them together, a tight, finely woven web. And he wasn't the heavy, vengeful spider waiting in the middle. He was the tiniest little fruit fly, wrapped up and left dangling on a sticky shivering thread, waiting now for the devastating gust of wind that was bound to come.

He had to put it behind him, he thought. He had to do it. From her ankles, he imagined his gaze rising, following the line of her calves, past the warmth of the backs of her knees, her skin almost glowing against the palm of his hand, and he continued to her thighs, trying to imagine grabbing her around the waist, but at the same time he felt sick from his own fantasy.

He was lying on his back on the mattress with his eyes open, following his breathing in and out, trying to calm his diaphragm. He concentrated on a patch of light on the ceiling. He let time pass without moving.

Finally he walked from the bed to his table, sat down with his hands on his lap, rubbed the middle of his left thumb with his right and waited for salvation that didn't come. He let more time pass, stood up, walked from the table to the window, then back again. And again. The yard was empty. And it stayed empty. He stood there a long time. The space hopper hadn't moved.

Sweating, he went down to the kitchen, where it was even hotter than upstairs. The air was so thick here he thought he'd suffocate. He had to leave the house. He had to go outside. To do what he was apparently predestined to do.

In the living room his mother was lying on the sofa softly groaning. "Jon? Where's my inhaler? Have you seen my inhaler? Could you get it for me?" He turned on the spot. It was too much; he couldn't cope with this too. In the kitchen he turned on the tap, splashed some water onto his face and rubbed it over his neck.

"Jon!" she called weakly.

But he turned the tap up full blast and put his head all the way under, letting his ears fill up with water so he couldn't hear her any more. There she was again, her voice coming through after all. "Jon? Are you in the kitchen?"

He squeezed his eyes shut and squashed his thoughts together so long and so hard until he'd shut out everything. He realized that if he just thought about her absence long enough, he could make her disappear. And himself too. It was like he was tumbling away, falling into darkness, but then inside, into himself. He felt his heart beating in his throat, as frantically as when he'd seen his own face lit up in the glass of the aquarium. Looking at that man in that reflective glass, at himself, who was that man, but also seemed to be someone very different. That man in the glass was going to do something he didn't have anything to do with. Briefly, that thought calmed him down. And together with an unreal relief, he felt a strange power growing within him. He had to leave, he had to go to her, there was no time to lose. He looked for the dog, whistled, walked down the hall and back to the kitchen, and found him in the yard. Asleep and quietly wheezing with his head on his front paws. When he whistled a second time, the dog raised his head for a moment, then lowered it again. "Come on, boy, come on now." He walked over to him. The sky above was gradually growing overcast. The weather was turning. Was it going to rain? He'd heard the forecast on the radio. Rain and squalls.

"Come on." Milk didn't respond at first; he just stayed lying there on the paving stones, then slowly raised his eyelids and had a scratch with his right hind leg. He twisted his head back and tugged at a scab with his teeth. "Come on, boy, let's go!" While making soft clicking sounds with his tongue and scratching the top of the dog's head furiously with the fingers of one hand, he used the other to attach the leash. It was already very windy. Above him wisps of cloud were joining together and racing across the slate-grey sky. In the distance a flock of seagulls was being scattered in the wind. Still no rain. Only heat. Heat that seemed like it would never go away, heat that pressed him down to the ground day after day.

He was smouldering on the inside too. The heat of his blood, boiling, his head broiling. It was punishment, he thought. Nature was punishing him. Or God. Jonathan didn't believe in God, but it still made sense that He would punish him. For what he was, for his thoughts, for his feelings.

"Now it's really going to happen," he said, shuddering. "It's time." Everything he'd wanted, everything he'd resisted for so long with all he had, now it was going to happen. And for the first time in ages he felt like there was only a now. No more past, no more future. As if time had swollen up, solidified and come to a standstill. As if nothing else would ever happen except this.

Tomorrow, maybe even this evening, the police would come to pick him up, he knew it. But no matter how much that scared him, he knew too that he wanted to reconcile himself to everything that was going to happen. The wheels will turn and they'll come for me, he thought. He'd fought and lost. Now all he could do was obey what was inside him.

Jonathan walked on without looking back and stopped just behind next door's. "You have to pee first," he told Milk. The dog relieved himself hastily in the sand behind the house and immediately walked on. The back door was ajar. They were still there. He had to act now. He could feel it in his breathing, high in his chest, fluttering, the tips of restless flapping wings, and saw himself going on, pulling the dog along behind him. Upstairs, he thought, just go straight up, don't stop to think. And you don't need to be scared of her mother. If you bump into her, he thought, you can just say something. Even though he didn't have a clue what he would say or how he would react, the thought of encountering her was no longer frightening. What could she do to him? She hadn't even looked after the girl properly; he'd like to tell her off. Where did she get the nerve?

Softly he pushed the door open and stepped into the utility room. He stood there for a moment and then walked further. Through the kitchen and into the hall. It was quiet. And empty. He stepped into the living room. He knew that the girl and her mother didn't have a lot of stuff, but this was worse than he could have imagined. Just like their house, but as if someone had taken away everything they owned and replaced it with junk. An old table made of unvarnished wood, a sofa covered with a stained bedspread. And everywhere the smell of damp. Dirty yellow rings on the walls. Piles of boxes stacked up in the corners. Dust floating in the beams of light. He walked through the low hall, with the same small panes as in their house, saw his own shadow, and continued up the narrow staircase.

"Hello?" he called. No answer. "Where are you?" It stayed quiet. In his thoughts he heard his own voice echoing briefly, then listened to the murmur of his blood in his temples. He quickened his pace. As he climbed the stairs it began to rain outside. The drops were tapping on the roof with a dull, steady rhythm and he stood still for a moment to listen. Rain with squalls, he thought, just like the forecast. He clenched his fists; his mouth was dry. It had to rain more. Roaring thunderstorms, gales tugging at him, at his body and limbs, shaking him in all directions, that was what suited how he felt, the fury inside him. But the falling of the drops, the tempo at which they splashed down, remained soft and calm. He bit on the inside of one cheek and then the other, made some chewing movements and felt more saliva appearing in his mouth, then climbed the last steps. At the top, he stared at the trembling dust particles floating in the light. They seemed to come out of nowhere, without any purpose. It was still so quiet that he realized he wouldn't find anyone. He walked on.

He stopped on the landing and looked around in the dim light, letting his eyes adjust before taking it all in. Bare walls, unpainted wood, a kitchen chair in the corner next to the door that must lead to her bedroom. An environment that told him nothing: anyone could live here, or nobody.

He found it hard to believe this was her house, the place she went back to every afternoon after they'd been together. Where she slept at night. He kept staring. There was something about the abandoned scene that bothered him: the longer he looked at it, the more he got the strange feeling that there was something the surroundings were keeping hidden from him, that there was something he wasn't allowed to see. As if the things, the shapes and the dust had made up their minds not to be caught out, as if they were holding their breath, waiting until he'd walked on, to only then show their true nature.

He listened to his own breathing. Studying the room, he flared his nostrils, but the smell he hoped to catch also stayed hidden. Her smell wasn't lingering anywhere. Now, when he was longing for her so intensely it hurt, she was further away than ever. Somehow he could only picture her in fragments too, in details. That smile, her tooth, her lips and the way they didn't entirely close, the fleck in her eye, the side of her neck when the late afternoon sun was shining on it. But these things wouldn't combine to form a whole. He had to go into her room, he thought. That was where she would be closest to him.

Her bedroom was small, just like his. Although hers seemed even smaller. The air inside was just as warm and muggy. Here too he could pace the length of the room in seven steps and the breadth in three. Half an arm's length up to the rafters of the ceiling. Where his table stood, there was a plastic box full of toys. The arm of the doll he'd seen so often before was sticking up over the side, together with one end of her skipping rope.

Where he had his bed, she had a small desk. And where he had his aquarium, there was a mattress on the floor.

Jonathan walked over to it, got down on his knees and ran his hands over the slightly greasy surface. He took the sheet that was draped over the mattress by the corners, held them together and brought them up to his nose. Yes, now, now he could smell her. He was immediately hard again. Sweat leapt out of the pores along his hairline. He wiped it away with the corner of the sheet.

Suddenly he felt an overpowering urge to have a wank— here, with all her things around him. The mattress on which the impression of her body was still almost visible, her table, her doll, her skipping rope. Just when he was about to unbuckle his belt, another memory shot off like a spring that had come loose in his head. She was sitting across from him with her eyes screwed up, and he heard her voice as she began to read the story she had just written. He was overcome by shame. It was too much. The blood was surging through the arteries in his head, swelling and stretching them. His skin was going to burst. No, he shouldn't wank here, it wasn't meant to be like that, he needed her with him, he wanted her, warm and sweet, against him. He pressed his eyelids with his fingertips and held them there, breathing very slowly through his mouth. "Where are you?" he whispered.

He wanted to leave but couldn't, not yet. After sitting still for at least a minute, he stood up, only to sink back down onto the floor almost immediately. He smelt the sheet and crawled over to the desk in the corner of the room. The exercise book she was always writing in was right there, open and arranged neatly in the middle of the table, surrounded by crayons, pencil stubs, a felt tip. The seat of the chair was covered with sheets of paper with writing on them. He pushed them over to one side to sit down.

He stroked the cover of the exercise book, which was opened at a page titled: "The secret mision. The club." In big, awkward block letters she'd written: "What we have to do to save Tinca." Under it there was a summary: "Water not more than 23 degrees, enough mud, quiet and snails (bythinia), that's her favourite food. You find them in the lakes in the sand dunes."

That was where she was. Of course. How could he have been so incredibly stupid not to think of it? Of course, she'd gone to get the snails.

He listened to the rain tapping on the roof. He pictured her in her shorts with a raincoat on over her top. Her limp, wet ponytail. She was wearing her wellies. In his imagination she made her way from the path to the edge of the lake, quietly talking to herself. Maybe she'd taken a bucket from home. Bending forward carefully, she poked a branch into the muddy water by the bank, scared to go too close.

Was the rain stopping? He wanted to see an opening in the clouds, pale hesitant sunlight caressing her face. He remembered how beautifully the light had shone on her throat and cheeks that afternoon at the swing and how she half closed her eyes while he pushed her. He could almost taste the greasy crisps he'd fed her, almost feel the oppressive heat, her eyes on him, the soft, parted lips he almost touched with each crisp, the movement in the dimple at the bottom of her throat when she swallowed. His heart was thrashing again and he put the film on pause, but it started rolling again almost immediately, opening, unfolding.

Her soft, parted lips. Him feeding her. And then he saw it happening. Very close. He grabbed her hair. As if to save himself from the whirlpool of his own thoughts. As if he could save her from the fire that was raging in him, around him, sucking everything in and burning everything to a cinder. But how could he ever insist that it was her safety he was after, because in his thoughts he was pushing her down on the ground. His fingers curled up, clawing. He smelt the cheap shampoo so deep in his nose he couldn't escape it. And there was the next moment. She was naked—he didn't even think about how he'd undressed her—in his thoughts she was already naked. He saw her legs and between them a shell of immaculate flesh. Now the film slowed down. He was kneeling before her and she was lying on her back with her head turned to one side. His tongue left a track along the inside of her calves; he pushed her legs apart. There was the pinkness and he touched it very cautiously, and he'd never felt anything like it, softer than everything else. Inside his head the film kept playing in slow motion. Silent but with vivid moving pictures. So vivid that he could feel her beneath him. He'd never permitted himself to go this far before, to see it in such detail, to feel it and not let the calmness inside him be interrupted by anything, as if it was all coming together.

He was inside that warmth, that softness. He changed position and wriggled his hand in under his belt, as if that way it wouldn't be him who was doing it, as if it would be her. He only had to move his hand a couple of times and he could already feel the driving warmth surging up from deep in his balls. But he squeezed and stopped it. Not yet. Not here.

He wanted to get up, but there was no stopping it. Not with her smell wafting through his brain, and the heat, and another inescapable surge came. She didn't look at him, just kept vaguely smiling. In his imagination she had the same distant look in her eyes as when she was reading. She was there, but at the same time she wasn't. She didn't see him. Not while he was inside her. She didn't make a sound. It was like he didn't exist. Suddenly angry he pushed deeper into her, spread her legs high, pushing them apart with his hands, thrusting and thrusting again and staring at her face, waiting for a twist of her mouth, something to show that she felt him, that he existed. But she kept stubbornly looking the other way. Almost crying with rage, he kept tugging at her in his thoughts. Surely in his fantasies he could at least get her to do what he wanted?

Look at me, he thought. Lift up your head. He tried to raise the girl's chin but she resisted. Her neck muscles stayed tense. He heard a rhythmic sound, the slap of flesh against flesh, as if this wasn't just in his head. Finally, she turned her head towards him. She smiled, but her eyes were gleaming sadly. And despite the victory of finally controlling her, he again felt a short, sharp pang of disgust. He ran his fingers through the child's sweaty hair and looked down at her again. Now she was looking at him from behind her exercise book. He thought of her head pressing against his shoulder, her mouth open, a faint smile, and he saw her blonde hair, her skin, everything that was so beautiful and perfect about her, the quiet little noises she made when she was writing. He gulped to swallow the snot and tears, but in his mind it was her eyes that were full to overflowing and the tears were starting to roll down her cheeks and chin. He stroked her throat and trailed his fingers over her cheek. "Hush now," he soothed.

The ceiling seemed to be lowering. He could see her sitting across the room, a silhouette, motionless. "Turn around," he said, but in this room all sound seemed to disappear into a strange silence. It couldn't end like this, him alone in this barren, godforsaken desolation—he had to break out of it. Alone. He had to get away from here, to her.

Suddenly he was outside again, in the steady rain, and he started running, the dog behind him. Jogging, but going as fast as he could, he skirted the village. Along the gravel path, the long dune path, climbing until a stab of pain in his heaving chest forced him down onto his knees. The wet sand and broken shells scraped his palms. Milk came round in front of him and started panting into his face. "Stop it." He pushed him away, spat a big gob out on the ground, coughed, wiped the moisture away from his neck, scrambled back up and started running again. Now through the small wood. The pines surrounding him reached up into the grey sky with their gently swaying branches. They were close together, cutting him off, no room to get through between the trunks. Sometimes he felt like someone was watching him; the next instant he was running towards freedom. The wind blew through the treetops, the murmuring rain drowned out the pounding of his blood. Branches snapped under his feet, he was kicking up pebbles, and sometimes he couldn't tell where the sounds were coming from, if he was making them himself. He tried to think, to follow a straight line in his head and through the wood, the shortest path to where he wanted to be. But he was thinking of everything at once and sometimes his thoughts stopped altogether, sinking in dark silence to the unreachable depths of his mind. Just before the clearing where he would get the first view of the pond, with less than five minutes' jogging to go, his lungs had had enough. He sat down for a moment on the pine needles, his back against a tree trunk. He rubbed his face, pressed his forehead and eyes, and thought once again about what was going to happen when he saw her, the fear of what he was about to do gnawing away at him.

Through the branches he could see the sky, which was still overcast. A suffocating layer of grey cloud. He stopped at the start of the path that led to the pond. The dog made a few low, growling noises, raised his nose in the air to sniff, then wanted to carry on. "Milk." He gave a short, quiet whistle. "Here." The dog obeyed and came shuffling back.

He was too scared to keep going. Together with the dog he stood indecisively in the hot air that had gathered round them like thick smoke. It was still raining, but the drops were feeble, as if they too had been reluctant to fall, suddenly mistrustful. He pressed the toe of his boot against a pile of sand, but it was solid and unmoving. The rain was trickling down from his hair in little streams over his temples and cheeks, without cooling him the way he'd hoped.

Slowly he turned left onto the last path, reached the clearing where it branched, and took the narrower track on the left that led east, down to the water. Soon he could make out the shape of the pond on his right.

He paused. In the distance he could see mist over the water. Now a terrible fear was upon him. Faced with the stretch of open ground that separated him from the pond, it was like his legs had stopped working. Then he moved one foot and felt like he was angling forwards, as if he would topple over an edge if he took another step. It was like a strong, unearthly gravity pulling him down, then pushing him up away from the earth. He didn't dare to look, not ahead, not back. He felt like lying down flat until it was over. Until it had blown over like a storm he could hear raging past, and only when the wind had died down would he stand up again, brush the pine needles off his jeans and look around. But nothing in his life ever passed over like that: they were just vain hopes. This too would not pass. He had to complete it. He had to go to her; he was almost certain she was at the pond. On the bank, whispering to a jam jar full of snails. He clung to that image. That was what it would be like, what it had to be like. He tried again to get his legs moving. He could feel the muscles of his face tensing up. Slowly he began to walk.

As if from an enormous distance he saw himself walking towards the water, back bent, shoulders hunched, staring at the ground. The longer he watched, the smaller he got. As if the world had cut him loose and he was floating through a cold universe like a tiny little planet. He raised his head. His gaze searched in all directions, as if he might still find someone or something, anything that could give him an answer, a place where he could lie still. Above him he saw a beam of light trying to pick its hesitant way through the clouds. He looked at it carefully. For a moment the pencil of light seemed to get stronger, but it couldn't break through the thick layers.

His jaw started to quiver. The little muscles around his mouth tightened. He struggled to hold back the tears and scanned the surroundings. The air was still sickly warm. Light, feeble rain was dripping on his face, his body. He sped up.

He walked round the east side of the pond. His mind was blank and overflowing at the same time and he walked as if there were two of him. As if part of him was leading the way, nervous, focused on the toes of his boots, while the other part hurried along behind, trying to see past him.

He couldn't see her anywhere. He walked purposefully; he knew where she would have got into the water. There was only one spot where the reeds were thin enough. That was where he was headed. And in the same instant he heard a sound of something breaking, a branch, and spun around to see if he was being watched. It was nothing. He turned back. His eyes began to scan the bank, casually at first, then faster, further into the water. First he didn't see anything, he didn't want to see anything, he let his eyes be guided by a tension he felt high in his throat, but then he forced himself to look more closely.

He approached cautiously and stepped into the middle of the slowly growing patch of light the sun had cast down through the clouds. Legs apart, rocking on the balls of his feet. He moved a little closer and then he saw it.

The girl was floating in the middle of the pond with her face in the water. Hair fanned out like seaweed, arms weightless, stretched out on both sides of her body. She was wearing her towelling shorts, her wellies and the top with the flower. It seemed like such a long time since he'd seen her in that top. A different life, a different person. Or at least he thought he was a different person then.

He stayed standing where he was, arms dangling awkwardly by his sides, his hands trembling. It was impossible to believe that it was really her. The girl. He couldn't say her name. As if that would somehow make it real.

Each time he thought of her name, it fell apart in his head. The letters and sounds detached from each other; the glue that held them together dissolved before he'd formed the word. Now you have to do something, he told himself. This is your fault.

He took a couple more steps in her direction. From this distance she looked so small, much smaller than she really was. He felt dizzy and knelt down, but even on his hands and knees he kept feeling like he could topple forward at any moment. He wanted to lie down. Stretched out. Sinking into the earth like it was a grave. But he couldn't leave her floating there like that. He had to save her, save what was left to save. He closed his eyes and shook his head hard, but everything in him was numb and solidified. Everything except the part inside his head that had him getting her out of the water and laying her down next to him. That was the only thing he could do for her.

"Here," he told the dog, who scratched his coat with his hind leg and didn't react. "Here!" His voice sounded as thin as a gossamer thread that could be blown away by the slightest hint of a breeze.

When Jonathan started to walk, Milk began to follow him with his slow lope. Together they walked a distance into the pond. Then Milk stopped and Jonathan walked on. The water washed over the top of his rubber boots. He felt the suction of the muddy bottom of the pond. Now and then he sank into a hole. But it only got deeper slowly.

After a while he could no longer see his boots, and the legs of his jeans were saturated. When it had risen to halfway up his chest and he had almost reached her, he thought in a flash that he could keep going. He screwed up his eyes. Keep walking, he thought, until the water comes pouring into your mouth and lungs. Until everything's over. But he wasn't going to let himself off like that, he hadn't earned it. Death would be too easy. He had to suffer, facing up to what he'd caused, and so he looked at the floating body, not less than four metres away, and thought of all the things he'd wanted to do to her. All his rage, the aroused fury he'd felt in his body, was gone. There was just a deep silence and a powerful but gentle longing to look after her.

He reached out cautiously, gripped her by the shoulders, pushed his hands firmly under her armpits and, shuddering, turned her body towards him. With one arm wrapped around her back and chest and the other supporting her chin, he lifted her face a little. A few tufts of hair were stuck to her forehead. Her mouth was open. Strangely, the expression on her face was no different from what he was used to seeing. It was just her eyes that he didn't dare look at. With his face averted, he used the thumb of his right hand to slide the lids down over the two eyeballs in which he, looking from the corner of his eyes, couldn't even see an edge of pupil. He brushed some hair away from her face and began pulling her through the water to the side. She was heavier than he'd expected. He started panting.

After reaching the reeds he took a step up the bank, dug his heels into the mud, slipped for a moment, recovered, gripped her with his arms around her back and pulled her up onto his shoulder. Again he was struck by how heavy she was. A few steps away from the water, he wobbled and fell face down and the girl landed on top of him. He lay there like that for a moment, the dead weight of her body on his, which was gasping heavily. If he could, he thought, he would stay lying there with her for ever.

But finally he pushed up with his back and the girl rolled off, falling on the sand with a thud. Now he lay down next to her, his breathing calmer. For a long time, a time he could never have measured, a time nobody could have measured, he stayed there stretched out next to the girl's unmoving body. Close enough to touch her with an outstretched hand, if he had dared.

I'm lying here with you, he thought. You're with me. That's all that counts. All he wanted now was to have her with him. "I did look after her well," he whispered with a choked voice, rolling onto his side. He leant on one elbow and looked down on her. Through his tears he saw her still, unscathed face, and let his gaze drift over it. She looked angelic, not puffed up at all, more beautiful than ever. "There you are," he heard himself say. He could only look at her. Carefully, without touching her skin, his finger brushed her hair to one side. Just stay lying here a little longer, he thought. Don't think. He knew he had to go. But in a strange, twisted way, he could finally breathe.

The dog was sitting right next to the girl's head and pressed his nose against her chin. A quiet, high-pitched squeak escaped his nostrils. It had stopped raining. There was mist hanging over the water of the pond.

"Here, boy." He took Milk by the scruff of his neck and pulled him over against his own body, gently scratching his head for a moment. Then he stood up, walked around the girl and sat down on the other side of her. He wanted to be with her so much, now it was still possible. Looking down at her hesitantly, he gently explored her face with his fingertips. He felt the loose hairband in her wet hair. He brushed her cheek lightly with his knuckles. He held an ear lobe between his fingers like a thin, flat pebble. Still inquisitive, the dog came over again to investigate the lines of her face with his quivering snout. Jonathan stayed calm and circumspect, but took him by the scruff of the neck again, hushing him and pulling his head gently towards him.

For a moment it was like nothing had happened, he thought, she was still here. But her mouth was drooping open to reveal a thick, fleshy tongue. He gently pushed her jaws closer together. The tooth with the chipped corner seemed smaller and so did her nose. The light shining down from behind the clouds struck the side of her face, lighting the corner of her jaw and her sweet, sharp chin.

He studied her face for a long time. It was the first time he was able to do so undisturbed. There was something strange about it, something wrong, looking at her like this when she couldn't open her eyes, but he couldn't tear himself away.

The very light, almost translucent shade of her skin made her face look even younger. All the things he hadn't understood about her were gone, they no longer existed.

And the things he didn't understand about himself didn't exist any more either. He had no strength left to think about things. Through his dejection, a deep calm had descended on him.

He looked up. A very thin quivering ray of sunlight was still stabbing through the clouds. Still. He knew this feeling wouldn't last, but now, for this moment, and at least as long as the light kept its distance and he was sitting here with her like this, he could live with who he was. The thick trees with their long, pale trunks stood around the pond like ranks of soldiers, keeping the rest of the world at bay.

He wanted to see the copper-coloured fleck in her eye in the light that would catch it so beautifully now, but he didn't dare to raise the eyelid he had just closed. Slowly, searchingly, he let his gaze slide over the rest of her body and kept finding places that caught his attention. In the pocket of her shorts he could still see the piece of chalk. It was partly dissolved and had left a round, lilac stain in the material. He saw the trashy ring on her index finger. And on the knuckle of one of her thumbs there was a wound he hadn't noticed before. Had she just scraped it on something? The idea that she might have injured herself when she was alone was suddenly too much for him to bear and tears leapt into his eyes. He bowed his head and tensed his hands, curling his fingers until they'd formed fists. He'd managed to control his tears so far, but now he began to cry silently next to the motionless body.

"You poor thing," he whispered with his voice choked. "You poor thing." And then, "Elke…"

He had to go and struggled to his feet, forcing himself to leave her, starting to walk, but looking back once again. Suddenly it struck him that she must be cold. He rejected the thought, but still took a few hesitant steps back, and stopped again. It was crazy: of course she couldn't feel the water soaking into her body from her saturated clothes, but it was something he had to do. And in a strange way he was also proud of what he was about to do, something he didn't properly understand.

With the tears still trickling down his face, more slowly now, and his shoulders shivering, he unzipped his raincoat, took it off, unbuttoned his shirt and peeled the vest under it from his body. He stood there for a moment like that, holding his clothes, heavy from all the water they'd soaked up.

"What are you doing now, Jonathan?" he heard his lawyer's voice in his head. This isn't very smart, he thought. The moment the police find her with your clothes over her body, you'll be a suspect. What would happen next, the thing he'd been so scared of all this time, seemed to no longer exist. A ship that had disappeared over the horizon so that he could only see the foam-flecked ripples in the water. This felt like the only possibility. This was the only thing he could do, the only thing that still linked him to her. The only thing that kept the bond whole.

So he walked up to her, and carefully draped the vest and shirt over her body. Then he pulled his raincoat back on, the material cold against his skin, and began slowly, reluctantly, to walk away. But after four or five metres he again felt the urge to go back to her, and pictured himself doing just that, lying down next to her again and pressing his cheek against hers, his nose in her hair as if that might warm her up. He shook his head. You have to go. Even if he had nothing to go back to. The move to the new house was in three days. His mother would be alone again; she would have to move by herself. It was over. He'd never get out again.

He turned to Milk. "Come on, boy." The dog wagged his tail and ran on, stopping to wait for him at the start of the sandy path with his mouth hanging open.

Jonathan took a few more steps away from her. The sun was now shining under the clouds and straight onto her, lighting up her face. It had something biblical, he thought. It reminded him of a picture of Mary he'd once found in the drawer of his mother's bedside cabinet. A faded print with a pale-faced Mary, but with a halo around her head so bright it almost glowed and seemed to have burnt a circle in the card.

He took a couple more steps and looked back again. With every step it became more difficult to keep her image close. He concentrated on his feet, on the path stretching ahead of him.

It had stopped raining, but the muddy clods sticking to his boots still dragged his heels back down towards the earth. Just before taking the path that led to the village, he stopped to stand still one last time. He closed his eyes, rubbed his face, pressed his knuckles against his neck muscles, opened his eyes again and turned his head a few times from left to right, quietly cracking his neck. He brushed his eyes with his forearm, but they kept on filling, over and over.

Without rain to hold them back, the birds were cautiously starting to chirp and whistle and Jonathan listened as they broke the silence with their distant, lonely notes. He pulled his hands back out of his pockets, slowly rubbed the knuckle of his left thumb with his right, and then, not even bothering to look around, walked the rest of the way back to what was still, for the moment, his home.

PUSHKIN PRESS

Pushkin Press was founded in 1997, and publishes novels, essays, memoirs, children's books—everything from timeless classics to the urgent and contemporary.

Our books represent exciting, high-quality writing from around the world: we publish some of the twentieth century's most widely acclaimed, brilliant authors such as Stefan Zweig, Marcel Aymé, Teffi, Antal Szerb, Gaito Gazdanov and Yasushi Inoue, as well as compelling and award-winning contemporary writers, including Andrés Neuman, Edith Pearlman, Eka Kurniawan and Ayelet Gundar-Goshen.

Pushkin Press publishes the world's best stories, to be read and read again. Here are just some of the titles from our long and varied list. To discover more, visit www.pushkinpress.com.

═══

THE SPECTRE OF ALEXANDER WOLF
GAITO GAZDANOV
'A mesmerising work of literature' Antony Beevor

SUMMER BEFORE THE DARK
VOLKER WEIDERMANN
'For such a slim book to convey with such poignancy the extinction of a generation of "Great Europeans" is a triumph' *Sunday Telegraph*

MESSAGES FROM A LOST WORLD
STEFAN ZWEIG
'At a time of monetary crisis and political disorder… Zweig's celebration of the brotherhood of peoples reminds us that there is another way' *The Nation*

BINOCULAR VISION
EDITH PEARLMAN
'A genius of the short story' Mark Lawson, *Guardian*

IN THE BEGINNING WAS THE SEA
TOMÁS GONZÁLEZ

'Smoothly intriguing narrative, with its touches of sinister, Patricia Highsmith-like menace' *Irish Times*

BEWARE OF PITY
STEFAN ZWEIG

'Zweig's fictional masterpiece' *Guardian*

THE ENCOUNTER
PETRU POPESCU

'A book that suggests new ways of looking at the world and our place within it' *Sunday Telegraph*

WAKE UP, SIR!
JONATHAN AMES

'The novel is extremely funny but it is also sad and poignant, and almost incredibly clever' *Guardian*

THE WORLD OF YESTERDAY
STEFAN ZWEIG

'*The World of Yesterday* is one of the greatest memoirs of the twentieth century, as perfect in its evocation of the world Zweig loved, as it is in its portrayal of how that world was destroyed' David Hare

WAKING LIONS
AYELET GUNDAR-GOSHEN

'A literary thriller that is used as a vehicle to explore big moral issues. I loved everything about it' *Daily Mail*

BONITA AVENUE
PETER BUWALDA

'One wild ride: a swirling helix of a family saga… a new writer as toe-curling as early Roth, as roomy as Franzen and as caustic as Houellebecq' *Sunday Telegraph*

JOURNEY BY MOONLIGHT
ANTAL SZERB

'Just divine… makes you imagine the author has had private access to your own soul' Nicholas Lezard, *Guardian*